PALADIN

THE VIGILANTE CHRONICLES™ BOOK FOUR

NATALIE GREY

MICHAEL ANDERLE

DISRUPTIVE IMAGINATION®

LMBPN Publishing
PMB 196, 2540 South Maryland Pkwy
Las Vegas, NV 89109

First US edition, July 2018

PALADIN TEAM

Thanks to our JIT Readers

Mary Morris
John Ashmore
Daniel Weigert
James Caplan
Peter Manis
Paul Westman
Micky Cocker

If We've missed anyone, please let us know!

Editor
Lynne Stiegler

From Natalie

For M and T

From Michael

*To Family, Friends and
Those Who Love
To Read.
May We All Enjoy Grace
To Live The Life We Are
Called.*

Coyopa had a reputation as a despicable hellhole.

The planet had disappointed nearly every species that had come upon it. At first glance, clear blue waters held a seemingly-endless archipelago of tiny islands, each with white-sand beaches and an assortment of lush green vegetation.

The islands, however, could and often *did* move with each major storm, so building was next to impossible. The rains were fleeting and unpredictable, and the vegetation that grew so quickly was poisonous to most species.

Every once in a while, some cult or other decided Coyopa would be the site of their idyllic return to nature. Nature promptly ate them and spat out the bones.

The Jotuns, however, loved it. The saltwater was just the right temperature for them, they didn't need to eat the vegetation, and they had their ships on standby so that they could escape if any particularly bad storms roared through. Plus, they had the amusement of watching the cults fall apart.

Otherwise, hardly anyone ever came there.

When twelve carriers appeared in the skies above Coyopa on a lazy summer day, therefore, it was cause for considerable comment. Procedures were followed. The Jotun Navy was alerted by encrypted message, and satellite trajectories were altered to give the Jotun Coyopan Guard an idea of what they were dealing with.

When the satellites were shot down, one by one, they realized it was time to evacuate. It didn't matter who they were dealing with; they needed to get out, and get out fast.

Surface cruisers were readied and sent skipping over the water toward each major cluster of islands. Jotun civilians piled into temporary suits and holding tanks that had laid submerged, ready to be lifted into the bellies of the ships.

Jeltor, a member of the Jotun High Command who was presently on vacation with his family, bobbed worriedly in the tank of his loaner suit and wished he had access to the encrypted channels. Who would send carriers to Coyopa, of all places, and why?

An alert message blared through all of the suits: "There is time for one pass of the ship. Tanks 1-8 will be picked up. Tanks 8-16, proceed with all possible speed to the submersible vehicles for evacuation."

"I don't like this," Jeltor's wife said nervously. At 348, Lillik was old compared to many species, but barely middle-aged for a Jotun. Her body displayed the faint turquoise flush it bore when she was worried. It disappeared when their children clanked over to them in the tent. She didn't want them to see her fear. "There you two are! Stay close. We're in one of the tanks that will be evacuated by air." To Jeltor, she added, "Who would attack this planet? There are no resources here."

Jeltor said nothing at first. He followed her line of reasoning. Most issues that involved attacks were over things like mines or forests, perhaps plentiful flora or fauna. Coyopa had proved definitively over the years that it had none of those things.

However, Lillik failed to take the next step in her reasoning. If the fleet was not here for resources, why else could it be here?

To make a point. To make a point by killing Jotun citizens.

And while the Jotuns weren't at war with anyone right now, Jeltor had a pretty good idea who fit the criteria of both having a fleet and wanting to make an example of people.

The Yennai Corporation had been unchallenged in this sector of space for years. They didn't really have a main industry. They just seemed to show up everywhere. They had their claws into many of the banks, even running a few. For a while, they had owned one of the largest munitions companies in any sector of known space. They traded in information, mercenaries, arms, drugs, slaves...

That was, until a human had taken their main base, killing both heirs to the company in the process. Barnabas had judged both Uleq and Ilia Yennai and sentenced them to death for their misdeeds. Koel Yennai, who had not been on the station, was still free.

Now no one could figure what the Yennai Corporation was up to.

But Jeltor knew that anyone clever enough to build

something so far-reaching in the first place had a plan—and he was very afraid that Koel had decided to make an example of Coyopa. After all, the Jotun Navy had helped Barnabas find the Yennai base.

A shadow passed overhead as their evacuation ship slid into place over the open water. Jeltor bobbed nervously in his tank while long arms came down to start lifting tanks into the hold.

Come on, come on, come on...

Other shadows streaked overhead, casting everything into flickering darkness and light, and the distinctive whine of defensive ships sounded as their engines primed for maneuverability in Coyopa's atmosphere. Jeltor was telling himself that it was just a patrol when one of the first missiles struck the water nearby.

Helpless, Jeltor watched as the shock wave rippled toward them. He grabbed his elder daughter and shoved her suit behind his, and Lillik did the same with their younger. It was all they could do. When the shock wave reached the holding tank—

The tank groaned and creaked, and a single crack spider-webbed along the side of it. The shock wave continued past on both sides of the tank, and Jeltor felt a pang of relief…and fear.

They had survived one blast, but it was unlikely to be the last.

The captain of the rescue ship must have reached the same conclusion. Heedless of protocol, the ship shuddered and began to rise into the air, tanks still hanging from the retractable arms. Unsecured in the tanks, some of them not even in protective suits, the Jotuns cried out.

Their fear doubled when the ship rose high enough for everyone to see the battlefield. The Jotun Coyopa Guard had scrambled every ship available to fight off the enemy, but their efforts were ineffectual. The carriers weren't descending. They, and what must be destroyers, shot missiles from their position in orbit while smaller ships darted down to harry the Jotun fighters and confuse the antimissile tracking.

As Jeltor watched, one of the antimissile measures streaked into the blue sky and impacted a warhead of some kind. The passengers in the tank cheered, distracted from the fact that they were in an unprotected and swaying tank high above the ocean, and Jeltor didn't have the heart to tell anyone that what they had seen was a meaningless victory.

Every system here was state of the art, but Coyopa was so small and unimportant that Jotun High Command had never put very much here in the way of defense.

And now they were paying for it.

The rescue ship banked, the tanks creaked, and Jeltor looked up as the ship's unsecured occupants screamed once again. The tanks were still retracting as fast as they could, but the arms weren't meant to hold them in mid-air while doing maneuvers.

He counted the seconds as they came closer to the shadowed interior of the ship. The fighters created a barrier from the missiles and smaller Yennai ships for them—it *had* to be them, because who else would do this? —but it was clear they could only hold on for so long. When the tank at last disappeared into the ship, Jeltor caught a last glimpse of a Jotun pilot spiraling out of control toward the water.

Be safe, he thought, but he knew that pilot was not likely to survive either the impact or the ensuing explosions.

As soon as the tank *thunked* into place and began to drain, Jeltor opened a channel to his wife and daughters.

"I need to go speak to the captain and offer any help I can. You be safe and strap yourselves in, okay?"

They all nodded, and his wife managed a brave smile for the children. Jeltor felt a surge of love for her as he clanked toward the bridge.

He found the place in disarray. The captain yelled orders, the communications officers calculated whether they should transmit them or pass through the information they were receiving, and a quick glance at the sensor arrays showed that the Guard was in complete disarray.

The captain glanced at Jeltor distractedly. "Who the hell are you?"

"Commander Jeltor Howauc." Jeltor looked around. "Do you want assistance, captain?"

He tried to be polite. There were few breaches of etiquette more severe than someone throwing a captain off the bridge of their own ship, after all. On the other hand, this captain was clearly outmatched, and Jeltor was worried that years guarding a sleepy vacation resort had dulled the male's reflexes.

The captain clearly thought the same, because he stepped away from his chair with a little sigh of relief.

"All right, let's get everything back in progress." Jeltor swung into position and hooked the loaner suit into the ship's information feeds. He winced. In his own suit he'd be able to modulate the flow of information better, but in this suit, everything seemed to be echoing around in his head.

He'd manage it. He had to. His children and his wife were in a hold downstairs.

He charted a path through the battlefield and fed it to the other evacuating ships, then studied the arrangement of Yennai battleships, comparing it to theirs.

"This is Commander Howauc of Jotun High Command." He broadcast the message to all ships. "I am taking command of this portion of the fleet, and I am ordering a retreat. *Jose* and *Nodred*, rendezvous at the following coordinates to retrieve submerged evacuation vessels. The rest of the ships—"

The explosion was so bright it washed all the screens out. The electronics on the bridge of the rescue ship flickered, and Jeltor had just enough time to picture the ship tumbling from the sky before everything came back online.

"Gods have mercy," someone whispered.

Three mushroom clouds climbed into the air from the archipelago, and from the sudden blinking lights on the fleet screen to the side of the room Jeltor knew that the bulk of the ships hadn't made it out.

He shook even as he ordered that the ship accelerate as fast as it could go. They had to get out of here, and if their opponents had more of those missiles…

"Sir, the enemy ships are disappearing off our sensors," one of the officers reported. He brought up the display. "Only one is left, and it's sending a message."

Jeltor hesitated.

"Bring the message up."

Koel Yennai's face appeared on the screens, and Jeltor felt a strange mix of satisfaction and grief. The Torcellan had lost two people, both of them murderers in their own right, and he *dared* to retaliate by killing thousands of innocent civilians?

When Koel began to speak, his voice was hard and furious.

"We are aware that the Jotun Navy gave assistance to a human operative, enabling him to kill my children. This will be only the first of many attacks on the Jotuns if my demands are not met. First, the Jotun operative who helped the human must be turned over to face the justice of the Yennai Corporation. My second demand—"

"Turn it off," Jeltor ordered. "Record it, but turn it *off*. That is for High Command, not for us."

He fidgeted as the crew obeyed and began their preparations for high-speed travel.

Jeltor told himself that they weren't staring at him. They didn't know *he* was the Jotun operative Koel had spoken of. How could they, after all?

But *he* knew, and he had never felt guiltier in his life. He had helped persuade the brass to give Barnabas aid, and now their citizens were suffering for it.

Barnabas. He realized with a stab of misery that someone had to tell Barnabas.

2

"Put your hands up. Yes, just like that. Now if I were to punch, you could bat my strike away with one if your arms." Gar gently pulled Tafa's arm up to demonstrate. "See?"

Tafa looked dubious. "I don't know."

"Of course, you don't. You haven't tried it yet." Gar smiled encouragingly. "Come on. Light on your feet, make sure you use the stance I taught you—yep, that one. Now we start a little bit apart, and...go!"

Tafa skittered sideways and Gar patiently circled opposite her, waiting for her attack.

"He's good at this," Barnabas murmured to Shinigami.

"He is." She nodded.

They sat on the sidelines, a game of chess forgotten between them as they watched Gar teach Tafa how to fight. Today Shinigami was dressed like Bethany Anne on a day off: dark jeans, royal blue Christian Louboutin shoes with their scarlet sole—Barnabas had asked why you would put red on the bottom of shoes and had been roundly told off —and a grey blouse that accentuated the color of her eyes.

Shinigami had been playing around with the avatar she projected into the corridors of the ship. At first her goal had been to make the avatar look as human as possible, complete with tiny mannerisms such as blinking and fidgeting.

Now she was learning to accessorize.

Unconstrained by comfort, any underlying physical appearance of her own, or physics, Shinigami materialized in a variety of different forms and outfits.

Barnabas was still trying to deduce how any of it correlated to her mood.

Right now she appeared to be contemplative, even approving, as she watched Gar and Tafa circle on the mats. Gar had been teaching Tafa how to spar all morning, and despite her complete lack of knowledge and his relative inexperience, he had not once lost his temper. Whenever Tafa made a mistake he went back to square one, telling her where she had gone wrong and how to do things correctly.

Barnabas was impressed. When he had first met Gar, the Luvendi had been determined not to take a single bit of responsibility for his actions. He had blamed the terrible things he did on his employer, and he had run away from Barnabas rather than ask questions.

Only a couple of months later, he had proved himself to be a valuable ally. What he lacked in experience he more than made up for in enthusiasm, and he'd developed the same slightly prickly sense of honor that Barnabas recognized in all his allies.

And in himself.

Really, the worst that could be said of Gar was that he took kung fu movies a bit too seriously.

As they watched, Tafa darted in and landed a flurry of punches on Gar's arm. She shot away again at high speed as soon as Gar even twitched, and he smiled after her.

"Sometimes it makes sense to retreat before the other person can hit you," he told her. "Sometimes you want to stay close and take the hit."

"*Why?*" Tafa demanded. She had been the one who wanted to learn to spar, and she kept at it with an admirable amount of determination. However, saying that it didn't come naturally to her would be a massive understatement.

Simply put, the Yofu were *terrible* at fighting.

"Well, say you were here, and I punched you—I'm not really going to punch you, don't worry. Yes. So you're here, and my hand is here. Now you see how there's an opening at my side because my arm is up."

"But I got hit," Tafa protested.

Gar's lips twitched, and Barnabas could sense him trying not to laugh or be impatient.

"Yes, but getting hit once makes sense if you think you can get something worthwhile for it."

"Oh, I don't get this." Tafa looked at Barnabas. "Is everybody this terrible at it to start with?"

Barnabas searched desperately for something diplomatic to say, and managed to come up with, "Everyone has different challenges at the start."

"Smooth," Shinigami murmured under her breath. She followed Barnabas' lead, though, and nodded at Gar.

"When he started, he was very inclined to go straight at someone, no matter the consequences. That was something he needed to change. *You* need to be a bit more assertive."

"But I'm *not* assertive!" Tafa wailed. She put her hands over her eyes. "I've spent my whole life trying to make people forget I was there. When it's just me and someone else in the ring, how are they going to forget me?"

"They're not," Gar said gently.

"I can't do this," Tafa muttered.

"Tafa." Barnabas smiled at her. "You know Gar, right? You've eaten with him, you've lived with him, and he's been teaching you to spar."

Tafa nodded.

"You know that Gar isn't trying to hurt you," Barnabas explained. "You were always worried about Mustafee wanting to hurt you, but he's not around anymore. He's quite dead. I checked."

Tafa managed a watery laugh.

"I'm not suggesting you take up a career that requires public speaking," Barnabas said with a smile, "but doing things like this that are a little uncomfortable makes us less scared the next time we have to do them. Right?"

"I-I guess?" Tafa looked uncertain.

"As uncomfortable as it is, I think sparring is good for you," Barnabas asserted. "Gar is an excellent teacher. Maybe you'll never be a boxer, but you'll learn something, and you'll be a better person for having faced your fears."

She stared at him, and he could tell she wasn't quite persuaded.

He pulled out the big guns: "Just imagine what sort of

paintings you'll be able to make with all these new experiences you're having."

Her eyes lit up, and she nodded enthusiastically. That decided it.

"Hell, yeah!" She bounced excitedly. "Let's do another round."

Barnabas nodded to Gar. *This should be interesting,* he commented to Shinigami and Gar with the implants.

She's not bad at any of it, Gar agreed. *She's just really tentative.*

I wonder what she'll be like with a little bit of self-confidence, Shinigami mused.

A moment later, her question was partially answered. Tafa launched herself across the floor at Gar, who responded on pure instinct. He slid to one side, swept Tafa's legs out from under her, and deposited her on her back on the floor with a thud.

His eyes went wide. "Tafa! I'm so sorry."

"*Ow,*" Tafa managed. She looked up at him for a long moment.

She's not injured, Shinigami reported after a quick scan.

A moment later, Tafa sat up with a grin slowly breaking across her features. "*That's* what I was so afraid of?" she asked them. "I was so scared of falling down, and *that's* all it was? I mean, it hurt, but..." She scrambled up. "Let's go again!"

Gar grinned wryly at her. "Let's see what you say after falling down for the twentieth time."

Barnabas was laughing when the message alert dinged. "It's Jeltor. Shinigami, should we take it on the bridge?"

"I want to say hi!" Tafa followed them, Gar at her heels.

They emerged onto the bridge in high spirits, with Barnabas wrinkling his nose at the smell emanating from Tafa and Gar. It seemed that there was a commonality between most species—when they sweated, it smelled terrible.

On the display, they saw Jeltor on the bridge of a surprisingly small ship, and his typically impressive powersuit had been replaced with something clunky and battered. Barnabas frowned.

"Jeltor. Is everything all right?"

"No," Jeltor said bluntly. "Just a few moments ago, the Yennai Corporation attacked Coyopa."

"It's a nominally-habitable planet on the edge of Sector 942," Shinigami reported. "Very close to 958. There's a *very* strange set of articles about… Not the time, I'm sure. Go on, Jeltor."

I think that was personal growth, Barnabas commented wryly.

Yeah, yeah. Laugh it up, fuzzball.

So…you don't like the beard? Barnabas touched his chin self-consciously, where there was the fine stubble of a beard he had been attempting to grow out. Shinigami's constantly-shifting appearance had inspired him to try new things.

I was trying to find a way to tell you. Not that it makes any sense for me to bother, though, since you clearly don't listen. Your hair is still red.

Auburn. It's auburn.

Call a spade a spade. You're a ginger.

Hmph.

The exchange had passed in a split-second, and Jeltor

was still trying to find words. "He wanted to make a point," the Jotun said finally. "Coyopa is a place that no one but Jotuns want, so I don't think there were any aliens. He was trying to punish us for helping you."

"Punish— Jeltor, why are you acting like it already happened?" Barnabas frowned. "You said it was just a few minutes ago. We're en route. Should we—"

"Don't bother," Jeltor expressed sadly. "There's nothing left. He nuked it. A few ships got out, mine included. Many of the rest..." He paused. "They were civilians, Barnabas. On vacation. There was only a nominal military presence there. He picked a target that couldn't fight back and he—" He broke off.

Barnabas' face was white with fury. "He attacked *civilians?*"

"He said it was justice for our Navy helping you. He's demanded they turn me over to face his justice as well. I... don't know what else." Jeltor gave a sound like a sigh, and his jellyfish-like body turned several brilliant colors before returning to its normal blue. "I stopped watching the message after that."

"You did the right thing," Barnabas said.

"I know. I know he had to be taken down—"

"No, I mean not listening to the message. From what little I saw in his children's memories, he's...not entirely sane." Barnabas shook his head, his eyes distant as he thought through the memories from Uleq and Ilia Yennai. "I don't think there's much to be gained from listening to him."

"All the same, could you send the message to us?" Shinigami asked.

Jeltor nodded. "I'll transmit it in a moment. In the meantime, I suppose I should go back to Jotuna and see what they want to do with me."

"What they want to—" Barnabas sputtered. "They're not turning you over?"

"They might."

"For the love of— We will meet you at Jotuna, then." Barnabas' voice was cold. "And I will explain to them that if they want to bow to the whims of a complete madman, they can turn *themselves* over, or no one. Koel Yennai is a megalomaniac. We are not bargaining with him."

Jeltor paused but bobbed in a way that Barnabas knew was similar to nodding. "I would be glad to have you speak in my defense."

"No defense is needed," Barnabas contended. "But I will be glad to speak to them, yes. I will see you—"

The klaxons wailed, and Shinigami flickered in her seat. When she came back, she was wearing armor—and a cold expression.

"There's a Yennai scout ship on our scanners," she reported.

"Jeltor, we'll have to call you back," Barnabas relayed hastily. He ended the call and nodded to Shinigami. "Let's get this scout ship before it gets word back to Koel."

3

Shinigami cloaked the ship at once. The term actually covered a whole range of technologies developed specifically for her. She'd be visible to sharp-sighted individuals looking out of particularly clear windows on ships that were very close to them, but otherwise, they would not be seen.

Which was good, given that they should almost certainly assume the ship had already seen them—

A moment later, she did not need to assume. The ship angled toward them and accelerated, weapons primed. The *Shinigami*'s scanners caught a budding electrical charge. The scout ship had intended to paralyze them, then call for help.

Shinigami maneuvered the ship up and over the trajectory of the Yennai Corporation ship, then flipped end over end so that the *Shinigami* was above and behind it.

Living organisms were predisposed to maneuver according to their idea of where "up" was. They liked rising above the plane of battle, as if they were still preoccupied with the idea of planets and gravity, and that ships should go "up" to fly.

Sometimes she wondered how these species hadn't managed to exterminate themselves before they ever got off-planet.

The scout ship slowed as it approached their last known point and fired two small missiles—the minor sort —to see if it could make the *Shinigami* swerve and somehow reveal itself.

It hadn't accessed its big guns yet.

"I have an idea," Barnabas said. He nodded to the image of the scout ship on their screens. "Would you be able to take control of its systems?"

"I don't see why not." Shinigami made her avatar shrug. "Of course...that does mean our cloaking won't work. They'll be able to see us with Mark 1 eyeball."

"You don't sound particularly worried."

"I'm not. It's just that we'll need to keep moving, and you and fish-boy there—" she jerked her head at Gar "tend to lose your lunches when the rollercoaster goes on for too long."

"That's all right," Gar said serenely. "We stocked up at the last station." He produced two air sickness bags and passed one to Barnabas. Gar opened his with a flourish. "Do your worst."

Barnabas gave a small sigh, but he took his bag without complaint. "Go on. I wasn't particularly attached to my lunch in any case."

"That's the spirit," Shinigami said encouragingly. "Attachment is the root of all suffering, you know." She smiled as she delivered the Buddhist principle, knowing that it would make Barnabas twitch.

It did. He tried to hide it, but she was an AI, so she could see the minute wince that passed over his face.

She chuckled as she zoomed in to follow the other ship. She drew up underneath it, signals tangling with its built-in protections, and felt a wave of amusement when the other ship jerked and swerved. Someone must have seen her from a turret.

"Idiot," she muttered. "He's got his hands on the controls while he's searching for us. Don't they have *any* sort of computer intelligence?"

"That's a question we should do our best to answer." Barnabas' voice was somewhat muffled by the bag. "It will inform our strategy. Whatever you find in his systems, make a note of it."

"I'm not like you, Chief. I don't just *forget* things I've seen." She swooped out of the way as the scout pilot tried to fire preliminary missiles at them. "Too slow!"

Gar made a noise like a distressed velociraptor and buried his face in the bag, and Barnabas wrinkled his nose at the smell.

Shinigami would have been more amused, but her attention was well occupied between her maneuvers and her attempts to get into the systems of the scout ship. Small as it was, it contained a veritable trove of both information and weaponry.

Its programs and offensive capabilities had clearly been designed by a ruthless and powerful organization. Whereas the purpose of scout ships was usually to find information and allow the rest of the fleet to deploy as necessary, this one also possessed the ability to kill mid-sized ships.

Shinigami thought of Koel Yennai's children, and of Barnabas telling her that Ilia had been ordered to kill Uleq. To her surprise, she felt sad. Koel had built his family and his organization the same way—as trained killers, all of them determined to show strength before anything else.

When had things like that started to make her *sad*?

She didn't have time to think about it. She flipped and fired countermeasures to evade another set of missiles, then returned to hug the top of the scout ship. It tried desperately to evade her. It might not know what she was doing, but it was determined not to let her do it.

It didn't have much of a chance. As it twisted and turned, banked sharply and flipped, Shinigami stayed right with it. She hacked her way into its systems slowly but surely until finally she disconnected the manual controls and swung the scout ship to face her. She held it, floating, and smiled.

Barnabas and Gar, both of whom had been doubled over their airsickness bags, looked up with interest.

"Just a moment..."

Shinigami worked her way into the messaging systems. There, in no less than three distinct places, she found embedded location tracking for any messages, as well as a subprogram that scanned and mapped any pulsars to send back.

That last one amused her. Humans had once done the same thing. They'd sent a tiny craft called *Voyager* out into the stars with a map of pulsars engraved on a plaque that would lead anyone who found it back to Earth.

It had been a remarkably hopeful gesture from a species that had decided to trust that the universe was more likely to be a good place than a bad one. Those who made *Voyager* had wagered—wagered with their descendants' lives—that it would not fall into the hands of anyone who would come and steamroll Earth.

Shinigami thought this was the stupidest thing she'd ever heard.

She didn't mention any of this to Barnabas, who would probably wax poetic about the power of hope and how the universe *wasn't* an inherently bad place. For someone who liked to think of himself as a jaded vigilante he really was hopelessly idealistic sometimes.

She snickered to herself quietly as she corrupted the data the messaging systems had attempted to relay back. Koel wasn't likely to think it was an *accident* the location tracking didn't work.

On the other hand, she didn't want to give him any more clues than she had to about her capabilities. Embedding random number generators and white noise into his data was a fairly basic technique, and something he couldn't reverse-engineer.

She nodded to Barnabas. "You're good to go in three… two…one."

Barnabas focused on the ship displayed on his screens. He wished he could see Koel's face right now. Something about the male unsettled him in a way few people did. The hint of madness behind the eyes, perhaps. Koel was an entirely rational, logical person…

After you factored in his completely sociopathic view of the universe.

"It's all beginning to come apart for you," Barnabas mused, "isn't it? You'd spent so long being careful, working from the shadows, and then as things began to accelerate, it all went wrong.

"You hold us responsible for the deaths of your children, perhaps. Yes, I was the one who ended their lives. But you were the one who raised them to be what they were. You were the one who terrified them into believing that you were a god, with infinite power over their life and death. Had I not been there, Ilia would have killed Uleq on your orders. You made both your children murderers. Do not rage at me for bringing them to account. Indeed, you have no one to blame but yourself for the fact that they are lost.

"Though I do not believe for one moment that you ever wanted your children to live their own lives and build their own destinies. You wanted them to glorify you, nothing more."

Barnabas paused. What *he* wanted was for the Yennai Corporation to be extinguished. He also wanted Koel Yennai to face justice.

And he wanted those things to happen with a minimum of collateral damage.

But what could he say that would not prompt Koel to kill more innocents? He did not even know what Koel's aims were. Perhaps the deaths of his children had spurred him to action earlier than he had planned. Perhaps he hoped to establish some sort of empire.

Barnabas needed to end this, and for that...he needed Koel to want to kill him more than anything else.

"You would never have succeeded." He scoffed. "Your

children were weak. They begged for their lives, and would have betrayed you in an instant if they thought it would save them. *That* is what you have built, Koel. Your underlings are like whipped dogs who cringe and cower for a single bit of kindness from you, and then when you need them most...turn on you.

"You will be destroyed by your own folly. You wanted power, no matter the cost to anyone else, and your legacy will be ruin and failure. It will be me they will remember, not you. It will be my name on the lips of billions. It will be *my* vision that shapes the universe."

Barnabas cut the connection.

"Your name will be on the lips of billions?" Shinigami asked him. "That sounds like your nightmare."

"I was going to say," Gar murmured.

Barnabas shrugged. "I couldn't think of anything that would piss him off more than to tell him that I was going to get everything he wanted." He shuddered. "Who in their right mind would *want* to be known by billions? He should have asked Bethany Anne if being in charge of everything brings any joy."

"You're making a logical error," Shinigami told him. "Bethany Anne doesn't enjoy power, because she's legitimately trying to make things better and balance the interests of her citizens. *That's* a thankless shit-show. If you don't care about them, though, and you can just trample all over them on a whim, power's much easier to handle."

"Ah, yes—the perpetual logical error of thinking that my enemies have even the dregs of a moral code." Barnabas sighed, then nodded meaningfully to the scout ship on the screens. "As much as I hate to say it, that pilot cannot be allowed to tell them where he found us."

Her face was cold and hard as she directed the missile that turned the scout ship into dust. At this range, with the ship trapped, they only needed one. She could have vented the ship, of course, but who knew what automated systems might remain in a Yennai Corporation ship?

No. Only dust was safe.

A thought occurred to her, and her avatar smiled. Human mannerisms were becoming second nature to her now.

"What is it?" Barnabas asked her curiously.

"Koel Yennai is dangerous," Shinigami stated. She looked at him. "Some enemies, you wonder if they can change. You wonder if you should offer them mercy."

"Like me," Gar interjected softly. Barnabas and Shinigami turned to him in surprise, and he gave a small smile.

"Yes," Shinigami agreed. "Like you." She nodded at him, then looked back at the screens, where the rubble of the ship tumbled and glinted in the light of the distant sun. "But he's gone out of his way—many times—to show that he will not change. That we should not make the mistake of trusting him, no matter how helpless we think he is."

She smiled again, a rictus that chilled both Barnabas and Gar to the core.

"The only possible thing to do with Koel is destroy him completely."

4

The bar at Huen Base was dirty and reeked of smoke. Zinqued's eyes burned as he threaded his way between the tables. There was one alien in particular he'd searched for and tracked through what seemed like an endless set of systems, and to find her *here*, of all places...

It was good that she was here, Zinqued told himself. If she were here in this absolute hellhole, she'd almost certainly hear him out.

After their last run-in with the *Shinigami*, his captain had decided to go on the straight and narrow. Paun had given up stealing, or so he declared. He'd gone off to join some religious order, and was probably weaving baskets somewhere. Or teaching underprivileged children how to juggle.

Zinqued didn't know the specifics, and he didn't care. What he *did* know was that he'd managed to buy Paun's ship from him and he'd gotten Chofal, the ship's engineer, to sign on with him as well.

Paun clearly hadn't thought it was a good idea to sell

the ship to Zinqued. He seemed to know that Zinqued wasn't done with his quest to find the *Shinigami* and steal it.

But no one else had wanted to buy the damned thing. The *Julentai* was a bucket of bolts, an old Torcellan Gav-class frigate that was held together with spit and a prayer. There were an abundance of deathtrap ships for sale. Paun's wasn't anything special, and he'd had no luck unloading it.

Zinqued had sold everything he had to buy the ship, but it had been worth it. He'd never owned his own ship before, and it was liberating. He could go wherever the hell he wanted, and take whatever jobs he wanted.

Sure, he'd promised not to steal anything anymore, but it was his opinion that promises you made to a creature with glowing red eyes and bloody teeth didn't count.

So, with the *Julentai* at his disposal, he'd started tracking down one person in particular. A person who knew something about the *Shinigami*...and who might want revenge.

He'd tracked her through four stations before he heard a whisper that she'd come here—on the straight and narrow as well—and taken a job in one of the many factories that produced a nutritional paste for the variety of aliens in known space.

It was a miserable job. The paste might be nutritious, but it was nasty. The factory owners usually used cut-rate ingredients, anyway. To keep the factories vermin-free they were usually on desolate moons like this one, so there was nowhere to go if you wanted to quit.

It was about the last place anyone in their right mind would go. By choice, anyway.

It wasn't long before he spotted her. She was a Hieto, just like he was, so she didn't make too much of it when he sat down next to her.

"Are you Tik'ta?"

At that, she looked up sharply. Her eyes were flat and hard. "My name is Hino. I don't know any Tik'ta."

"Sure, sure." Zinqued smiled. "Just like you never tried to steal a ship called the *Shinigami* and watched your captain and crew get killed."

"I don't know what you're talking about. I'm Hino. I'm just another factory worker here."

"I saw you telling the story of the heist," Zinqued said, amused. "On Uto, not too long ago. Someone brought up that they'd seen a human ship, a pretty thing with a new paint job named *Shinigami*. You told everyone to not even try to steal it. You said it was owned by a demon and that he'd killed your captain."

She gave up trying to pretend that she didn't know what he was talking about. "*Fine.* But not so loud. Here, I'm Hino. I have to keep this job."

Zinqued saw the bitterness in her expression. She was penniless now. What had happened to her after he had seen her on Uto?

"You sold the ship," he guessed.

"I had to." She looked at him bleakly. "Stealing ships was all we knew how to do. We wanted to try smuggling, but we weren't sure if he'd find us and tell us we couldn't do that either. Some of the crew left, they were so scared. Nothing good to smuggle, anyway. You couldn't step on anyone's turf without them coming after you. And when we tried to go straight, there were permits and certifications and deposits and—and *bribes*. We tried to do what he said, but it was impossible!"

"He ruined your life," Zinqued said smoothly.

She glared at him. She wasn't about to be tricked by the fact that he said what she wanted to hear. "What do you want? Why'd you come to this hellhole to find me? I'm just going to tell you the same thing I tell everyone: don't try to steal the *Shinigami*."

"Because he told you to say that."

"He was right!" She shook her head. "Steal whatever other ship you want, but the *Shinigami* is death if you try. You didn't see what he did to our captain, Klafk'tin."

"I know." Zinqued had dealt with Klafk'tin back in the day. He tried to come up with something complimentary to say and failed completely.

For the first time, Tik'ta smiled. It was a conspiratorial smile. "I know what you're thinking. He was a son of a bitch who deserved to die. D'you know, the ship was booby-trapped, and he told the *Shinigami's* captain that he'd just keep sending us in because he was sure he had more of us than there were booby traps."

Zinqued whistled. "Not exactly going for the captain of the year, was he?"

"No." She laughed. "To tell the truth, I'm not exactly sorry he's dead. I thought he was just a run of the mill miser. He was arrogant. He kept trying to lower our salaries or make us pay for our food, stuff like that. But then he just said, cool as you please, that he'd kill as many of us as it took to steal that ship, and he *meant* it. That changed everything. I wasn't sorry Barnabas killed him." She shuddered. "All the same, you didn't see it."

"I saw the same sort of thing, though." Zinqued leaned close. "The Yennai Corporation hired my crew to steal the *Shinigami*."

"No! Yennai?" She leaned in as well. "To tell you the truth, I think something's up with them."

"Oh?" He might know a thing or two about that, but he wasn't going to tell her yet.

"Yeah." Her voice dropped even lower. "They're one of our biggest clients. Well, they're one of *everyone's* biggest clients lately. You thought they were big already? Well, in the past months, they've been buying *everything*. You name it, they're trying to corner the market on it—including politicians. More than they used to be."

Zinqued nodded. He hadn't known about the Yennai Corporation's sudden growth, but it had been clear for a while that they'd had designs on any number of industries and governments.

People who stole ships tended to be well-versed in the political goings-on of their sector. Certain governments were more likely than others to make a big deal of waylaid cargo—Get'ruz Shipping had discovered that the hard way about the Jotun—and anytime a new flag or ship designation showed up, ship thieves collected all the information they could.

They could have told people years ago that the Yennai Corporation was bad news...if anyone had asked.

No one ever did. Not even the information brokers realized what a goldmine of information was sitting right under their nose.

Their loss.

"They hired us for a big job," Tik'ta continued. She

gestured at the rest of the factory. "Only then they disappeared. The money never came through, and we have a bunch of parts we made, nowhere to ship 'em, no communication, nothing. Management's panicking."

Zinqued smiled. "Let's just say, they met Barnabas, too."

Her eyes got wide.

"Yeah," Zinqued said. "He doesn't just kill ship captains when they piss him off, he kills... Well, you want my guess? He killed Ilia Yennai. That's my *guess*, I said—I didn't see it. But she was one of the ones running the show. The big guy's daughter, yeah?"

Tik'ta nodded in understanding.

"Real piece of work, too," Zinqued said. Now that he wasn't there anymore he could joke about it. "She hired us, and she was going to off us after the job."

"And he killed her before she could?" Tik'ta was wide-eyed. She clearly enjoyed the conversation. To a ship thief, the flow of information was absolutely vital.

And anyway, who didn't enjoy a bit of gossip now and again?

"That's my guess," Zinqued repeated in a tone that said *but we both know I'm right.*

He didn't mention the part where he'd nearly fallen for Ilia's tricks. He'd survived and learned a valuable lesson. He was grateful to Paun for that.

That and the ship.

"Anyway," Zinqued leaned in, "if they've just disappeared..."

"They have. They *definitely* have."

"Then I'd say they're on the run, and *he's* chasing them."

"Why do you say *that*?"

"I don't think he's someone who leaves a job unfin-ished." Zinqued thought back to his meeting with Barnabas and shuddered. He'd been playing a part for most of this conversation, trying to get Tik'ta to sign on with him. She was a legendary pilot among the loose collective of ships they knew, and if they planned to steal a ship like the *Shinigami*...

They needed her.

Just then, the end-of-break bell rang and the foreman bellowed for everyone to get back to work. Tik'ta glanced over her shoulder, annoyance and worry imprinted on her features, and Zinqued made his move.

"Got a job for you."

She looked back at him, and the expression on her face was half mistrust, half hope.

"Just got my own ship," Zinqued continued. "I have a hell of a mechanic, and now I need a proper pilot. You should see *me* try to land that thing."

Tik'ta gave an unwilling laugh. Still, she knew enough to be wary. "How you gonna pay us?" *What kind of jobs are we going to be pulling,* that meant. She hesitated. "He told us we had to stop stealing things."

"And we will," Zinqued agreed easily. He smiled. "As soon as we got the *Shinigami*. We'll never have to pull another job again after that. All of us can retire for good. Mansions, servants, you name it. The Yennai Corporation wanted that ship. Who else would?"

Her eyes were wide and furious. "You're crazy," she hissed at Zinqued. "All of that, and what you took from it was that you should steal the ship? You said he doesn't leave a job unfinished! You said he managed to kill one of the big people in the Yennai Corporation!"

"And now he's going after the boss, who has a fleet…" He gestured to show just how big the fleet was. "You want to know my bet? Neither of them is going to win that. We nip in there at the right time, we can get that ship and be gone without anyone being alive to chase us."

She narrowed her eyes. "I have to go."

"Go where?" He looked at the doors of the factory. "Go make more food paste for a corporation that won't pay?"

She wavered. Zinqued could see that she was afraid. Her memories of Barnabas were too fresh.

That told him which way to go. "When Barnabas is dead, who's gonna care what you do with your life, anyway?" he asked her.

That got her. She tried to resist, but he knew he'd said exactly what she wanted to hear.

Finally, she nodded. She grabbed her badge, caught the foreman's eye, and threw it at his feet.

"I quit," she called across the room. She nodded to Zinqued. "Let's go, then."

5

K oel Yennai sat in the state apartment of his flagship, the *Avaris*, and watched the holo of Barnabas' message to him.

"You will be destroyed by your own folly," Barnabas said. "You wanted power, no matter the cost to anyone else, and your legacy will be ruin and failure. It will be me that they will remember, not you. It will be my name on the lips of billions. It will be my vision that shapes the universe."

The message ended and Koel fumed, consumed by a cold fury.

Barnabas' vision? What *was* his vision for the universe? It was nothing. It was dust. It was an acceptance of the way things were, using the false ideals of "peace" and "stability" to chain everyone who dared to reach for more.

Fuck peace. Fuck stability. The universe was constantly in flux. Koel didn't give a damn if some peasant's family had been farming on a little backwater moon for eight generations. If they stood in the way of his vision for the universe, they would get crushed.

That was what happened in this universe: you made the rules, or you were subject to them.

And Koel would *never* be subject to anyone else's rules. He would never accept things the way they were.

While others schemed to work their way up in governments or militaries, Koel had dared to reshape the entire sector. The others limited their dreams to the companies and governments they knew; the most enterprising ones started companies of their own, but such dreams were small—at most, they wanted to control a single industry.

His lip curled in contempt.

None of them, not *one* of them except him, had shown the vision to create something like this. And that didn't even take into account the patience it took to see his plan to fruition. He had spent *decades* finding allies, fronting them small bits of money, gathering information.

He had been poised to run this entire sector. Not directly, no. It was much better that way. No citizens to answer to directly, no major battles. While governments fought over territory and mining rights, Koel bought stock, subtly directed parliamentary proceedings on half a dozen different worlds, then sat back and collected a cut of the wartime profits.

He didn't have to worry that his tax revenues would go down or his territory would be seized. No squabbling board of directors or rogue political faction reorganized his budget. He answered to no one.

Soft power was enough, and he prided himself on that, too. It took discipline not to try to exert too much pressure. Most people wanted others to *know* they were in charge, but not Koel. He allowed other people the illusion of being at the top of the pyramid.

They didn't realize that the whole fucking pyramid was a lie.

He'd been within striking distance of having everything he wanted, too. And then...

Humans.

His whole body jerked with agony. His wife was long-dead; Ilia and Uleq had been all that remained of his family, and now they were gone, too. They had been stolen in an instant, leaving him with...

Pain. He would not admit it, except that it nearly crippled him. Before this, he was a fixture on the bridge of the *Avaris*. He gave the orders and directed everything. Now he was confined to his cabin; he could not let them see him like this.

But they knew. When he thought of his children, he could not stand, he could not speak. He could hardly breathe.

They were gone. He had known he would lose Uleq, but *this*? This was worse than he had dreamed. One pale hand splayed across his stomach as though he were cupping a wound, pressing over a growth inside his body.

The humans had stolen everything from him.

In the end, Uleq had been right. Koel had chastised him and called him a fool, but his son had been insistent. Humans were a threat to everything Koel had built. They were resourceful, Uleq had reported. They had impressive tempers, and yet they retained the capacity to be cold and calculating as they planned.

And their technology was more advanced than nearly every species in known space.

Koel hadn't worried or cared. The Yennai Corporation was hidden. It wasn't a government, with laws the humans would care about.

He had been wrong, and he had paid dearly.

My children—

He lifted his head, panting with pain.

He forced himself to stand although his muscles trembled, and he feared that he lacked the strength to do so. He took one shuddering step toward the window, then another.

His entire adulthood had been spent in this never-ending dance of sacrifice and gain. When the children were still young, his wife had begun to argue with him. Once his greatest supporter, she had started questioning his methods and his motives.

Isn't it enough yet, Koel? Can't you rest yet? We have more than we could ever need.

She did not understand, and when she threatened to take the children and deprive him of his legacy…

Well, what choice had he had but to kill her? It had been quick. He wasn't a monster, after all. And he hadn't lied to the children, either. He had explained it to them openly.

Lies could create such bad feeling.

He had sacrificed Avaris, the woman he loved most in the universe, for the future of the Yennai Corporation. He had named his flagship for her and remembered her fondly. How much more had he given up over the years as well? Reserves of cash, favors called in, ships and planets sacrificed, all for greater gains.

Now he'd lost the children, and he was certain he had never lost anything of more value than that. He would *find* a way to turn their deaths to his advantage.

He linked his hands behind his back and took a deep breath. For the first time in weeks, he felt like himself. Blind rage had driven him until now. He'd sought vengeance, not profit.

Finally, he was emerging from the fog.

He needed to keep a clear head. He had been willing to sacrifice Uleq to make Ilia stronger, so if he sacrificed them both...

He must, himself, become stronger. He would make use of this as he had made use of everything else. Had he not personally sacrificed Avaris?

Yes, this was an opportunity.

He went to his computers and started to research. Barnabas had given him a gift; Koel only needed to find it. He pored over information about the humans and their defeat of King Yoll, the abolition of the Yollin caste system, and their battles against the Leath and the Skaines...

It was well into the night before Koel sat back in his chair. The ship was down to its usual overnight skeleton crew, but he felt as fresh as if he had slept all night.

The power he had felt slipping away would be within his grasp again soon.

And this time, no humans would stand in his way.

6

"Shinigami," Barnabas said. "Can you research something for me?"

"Sure. I'm just landing the ship and negotiating with the Jotun high command. Why *not* add something more?"

Barnabas glared. "You know very well that half the time when I ask, you get very snide about the fact that you have almost infinite processing capabilities and can do as many simultaneous tasks as you want. You can go with that *or* the whole put-upon act, but not both."

"Why not? Meet me in the middle, here."

"I *am* meeting you in the middle." Barnabas cast an annoyed look at the speakers. "Neither of those is accurate. You get one lie. You can content yourself with the fact that it pains me."

Shinigami's avatar flickered into being, dressed in jeans and black Christian Louboutins. She smiled smugly. "That last part *does* help. So what was it you wanted to know?"

Barnabas had to pause to remember. "Ah, right. Why

are the names of so many species so close to the names for their home planet?"

"Oh." Shinigami nodded. "Most species' names translate in the original language to 'Earthers,' or whatever the equivalent is. For the Jotuns and the Luvendi, it would be 'Oceaners,' for instance. Almost every planet is named some variant by the species who live there. When they go into space they tend to get named by the other races, using their home planet's name. Humans are one of the only exceptions."

"I wonder why that is?"

"If I had to guess, I'd say we distracted them by showing up with a Kurtherian-tech fleet. They didn't spend any time coming up with nicknames for us after that."

"I suppose that would do it." Barnabas adjusted his cuffs. "Okay, next question. Will having either a Luvendi or a Yofu with me be *good* for this meeting, or should I go alone?"

Shinigami hummed slightly as she sorted through her data. "I'd say go alone. The Luvendi have a reputation as insular and money-grubbing bastards who will do anything to get ahead. The Yofu make good mechanics and have a fairly good relationship with the Jotuns, but unless you think Tafa is going to be a good diplomat, I wouldn't bring her. At worst they'll look down on her like hired help, and at best they'll assume she's your technical advisor and try to get her to spill details of your ship. Either way…"

"She's right." Tafa came around the corner with Gar. "The Jotuns are stuck-up bastards. Most people don't know it, because they tend to keep their heads down. They only deal directly with merchants and don't try to conquer planets or anything. Coyopa was different; no one wanted that place. But if you *do* deal with them a lot, you learn they think they're better than everyone else."

"Which would make Barnabas one of the few people they'll treat with even a modicum of respect," Gar agreed. "No one knows the extent of human capability, they just know it's broad."

"Hmm." Barnabas nodded. "Well then, we'll leave Gar and Tafa here." He gave them all a hard look. "You remember the rules, right? You *tell me* if someone tries to steal the ship."

There was a chorus of agreement and Barnabas narrowed his eyes. His team did not have a great track record when it came to reporting those things.

When he emerged onto the landing pad, it was a beautiful day on Jotuna. The landing pad was set a little ways back from the beach, but close enough that a sea breeze still stirred the air. Tall trees waved in the air, their bark ranging from brown to purple, and their brilliant pink and orange blooms nestled amongst the thick, glossy leaves.

There was a very faint clanking sound, and a Jotun in a powersuit made its way across the landing pad to speak to Barnabas.

"Ranger One, it is an honor."

"Thank you," Barnabas replied. "However, in the interests of accuracy, I must tell you that I am no longer Ranger One. I do not want to trade under the auspices of a government for which I no longer work."

"You may not work for the former Etheric Empire any longer, but it would be foolish for us to assume that you are no longer a part of their organization," the Jotun said simply. "No intelligence suggests you are no longer their ally. In fact, quite the opposite."

It was a warning, which Barnabas accepted with a wry smile.

He suspected that they knew why he was here and wanted no part of it, but they'd have to try harder if they wanted to intimidate him...or get him to back off.

He returned the warning shot with an easy smile. "I believe Jeltor's trial is in session. Take me there."

They stared at one another for a moment, human and Jotun. *I know more than you want me to,* Barnabas' expression said. *Don't make the mistake of treating this as a request.*

The Jotun finally turned and led the way across the landing pad without a word. Barnabas wished again he could read Jotun facial expressions. He had spent enough time with Jeltor to have some ability to read Jotun thoughts, but they still came through confused and murky to him. Speaking with such featureless aliens showed him how much he was used to reading emotion from facial expression and posture as well as thoughts.

Barnabas had set down right next to the Jotun government offices, so they didn't have far to walk. The Jotun led him along a spiral path into a subterranean building. Seawater had been channeled into raised glass-walled canals the Jotuns could swim through if they did not want to use the paths.

Barnabas understood that the Jotuns were proud of their powersuits and relished opportunities to use them.

Jeltor's trial was taking place in what Shinigami had guessed were the main parliamentary chambers. They had puzzled over the structure and rules of the parliament and come up with the idea that it might be democratically elected—according to incredibly arcane rules that Shinigami had struggled to translate.

The room was shaped like a bowl, with an open space at the bottom for the speaker and row upon row of senators at desks that lined the sloping sides of the room. No one here used tanks. Instead, they wore powersuits. Barnabas wondered if that was so they were able to use things like voting mechanics, which might be more difficult from tanks without arms.

Still, the sea was represented here in little streams that ringed the floor of the speaking area and waterfalls that Barnabas heard rather than saw. The air smelled alive, and faintly of salt.

It would have been very pleasant if Jeltor hadn't been standing in the middle of the bowl, clearly being grilled by angry senators—who, in Barnabas' considered opinion, had no right to question the Jotun's methods or goals.

There was a stir when Barnabas appeared. He took full advantage of it and walked to Jeltor's side.

"They have you on trial, then. What are the charges?"

"Treason," one of the Jotun senators asserted.

"Is that so?" Barnabas arched a brow. His thoughts ranged between this being hyperbole and wondering if they were really so far up their own asses that they believed it.

"Yes," Jeltor agreed simply.

Up their own asses, then.

"Explain the charges," Barnabas ordered them. He pitched his voice to fill the whole room, then he waited.

One of the senators closest to the floor shifted in his powersuit. He seemed annoyed at Barnabas' intrusion, but he was only too happy to list why he believed Jeltor was a traitor to the Jotuns.

"Commander Howauc is charged with unsanctioned aid to a military operation against an ally," the senator said shrilly. "His actions directly resulted in the loss of a Jotun colony."

"You refer to Coyopa," Barnabas clarified.

"Yes."

"I thought Koel Yennai's actions led directly to the loss of Coyopa."

There was an angry murmur and more mechanical squeaking from the senator. "He was, quite naturally, angered that one of our military personnel had helped assassinate his two children."

"He killed thousands of unarmed civilians," Barnabas shot back. "Additionally, I highly doubt that your legal code allows a corporation to be an ally. Furthermore, Jeltor had been captured by the Yennai Corporation and was being held so that he could be sold into slavery—an act of aggression against the Jotuns on the part of the Yennai Corporation. The fact that he participated in a fight of self-defense should not weigh against him."

The senators started to mutter amongst themselves.

They were live-streaming the trial, Shinigami reported, *but as soon as you started talking, they shut the cameras off.*

Of course. You can't have the common people hearing the truth.

Mmmhmm. Although I really should have said that they thought *they shut the cameras off.*

44

Shinigami, you're priceless. I'm giving you a raise. What do AIs get paid in?

Robotic bodies.

NO.

"Regardless of any *provocation*," the senator's voice dripped with derision, "Commander Howauc engaged in an unsanctioned military exercise. He did not seek permission."

"That is also incorrect," Barnabas rebutted calmly. "He communicated several times with the Jotun high command."

The senator laughed derisively. "And they are also on trial, Ranger One."

"This is a farce." Barnabas' temper started to rise. "You know that the reason you are in this mess is that you failed to contain a threat to Jotun interests."

"We are in this mess because Commander Howauc and his fellow officers betrayed our interests!" The senator slammed one mechanical hand on the table for emphasis.

Interesting, Shinigami commented. *People in robot suits do that too. Who would have guessed?*

I think he's trying to be intimidating. Barnabas tried not to shake his head. *And instead, he's just a coward.*

"Your *interests* were the bribes you took from the Yennai Corporation," Barnabas accused. "You personally took several years' worth of your salary in bribes this year alone, but you've been on their payroll for a decade, advancing *their* interests. You're scared now that they're angry, but ask yourself...why are they so strong in the first place? How did they get strong enough to destroy a colony, hmm?"

There was a ringing silence.

"Oh, yes," Barnabas told them. "I know exactly what each of you has gotten from the Yennai Corporation. I know how you voted after you received that money, and I can prove it. So here's my deal to all of you: I'm going to go destroy the Yennai Corporation. While I do that, you are going to halt this ridiculous trial excoriating Jeltor and the rest of the Navy. When I get back, *if* that demand has been met, I will *consider* going easier on you regarding the other demands I will make at that time."

There was a pause.

"You do not get to make demands of us," the senator blustered finally. "Someone must pay for—"

"Careful, senator." Barnabas' voice was cool, "or *you* just might end up being the person who pays. I can't say I'd mind that. And let me tell you—if you're betting that the Yennai Corporation will win and I won't be able to ruin all your careers? You're very, very wrong."

He nodded to them, a clipped, angry motion, then strode for the door. At the edge of the room, however, he paused.

"And should I learn that *anyone* has come to harm as a result of this ridiculous trial, be it one of the accused or any member of their families, I will make sure every Jotun knows how you have profited from their pain."

7

"It's really the only way," Barnabas said a few hours later. He leaned against the back wall of the conference room and chewed his lip as he examined the board. "Otherwise, he'll certainly find some way to cause as much collateral damage as he can."

"Are you sure about that?" Shinigami appeared, this time in a long black evening gown.

Barnabas blinked at her.

"I was just trying something." She shrugged. "I don't think I like it, though. It feels useless."

"Sure. And the high heels you've been wearing are... functional, somehow?"

"A bold accusation from a man with several hats in his closet—which, I might add, he doesn't even wear."

"Because you would make fun of me," Barnabas muttered under his breath. He gestured to the screens. "And yes, I am sure about Koel."

"What does he gain from it, though?" Shinigami asked reasonably. She laid one arm along the back of the couch and curled her legs under her. A moment later, with a muttered expletive, she disappeared and returned in her armor. "Much better."

"Although no more suited to the situation at hand," Barnabas pointed out, amused.

"I like armor."

"And you, unlike the rest of us, do not have to deal with the fact that it's immensely uncomfortable to wear."

"Yeah, I *really* like that part." She grinned at him. "If there's one thing Koel Yennai is good at, it's profiting from events. Using them to his advantage. He's not going to expend a bunch of munitions on random bystanders unless there's a damned good reason to do it."

"Well, for one thing, anyone even barely acquainted with me knows I hate the idea of innocents being hurt." Barnabas raised his eyebrows. "So it stands to reason that he would try to hurt them to get back at me."

"You're being awfully self-centered."

"I also poked a very vengeful bear with a stick, so to speak, to make him furious at me. First, I killed his children, then I taunted him about it. I am *not* coming off well in this conversation, am I?"

"Not very, no."

Barnabas sank onto the other couch and shrugged. "If anyone asks about it, I'll send them a list of Ilia's accomplishments. I'd think that would win me a reprieve from most people."

"Charming chip off the old block, that one."

"Yes. And more to the point, when it comes to him, I think we may have made him more dangerous than we meant to." Barnabas sighed and rubbed his head. "I wish we'd known more about him before we went to the base."

"What d'you mean?"

"I *mean* that his legacy was everything to him. He's an absolute sociopath. He was willing to have one of his children murder the other just to make her stronger so that she could run the company well when she took over from him."

"Didn't kings and queens on Earth do that?"

"That's apocryphal, and the point of such things was just to determine which was the strongest, not... You know, this is not important. It would be disturbing in any event. The point is that Koel Yennai is not entirely sane, has zero compunctions about hurting people, and we just took away the one thing he cared about."

"That won't stop him for long." Tafa stood a bit awkwardly in the doorway. She looked at Shinigami and Barnabas. "Can I come in?"

"Of course." Barnabas was surprised. So far, he had not attempted to include Tafa in any planning or discussion. She was on the ship while she decided what to do with her life, and mostly, she spent her time painting.

"You know Koel Yennai?" Shinigami asked dubiously. It wasn't out of the realm of possibility, after all. Tafa's cousin Mustafee Boreir had once been one of Koel's employees.

Until Barnabas killed him.

Tafa gave them both a wry smile. "I don't know Koel, but I knew people like him. Mustafee's mother was very similar. She suffered a lot over the years that I knew her. She lost people she loved, she had setbacks in the business, and her husband left her, but she didn't respond the way any normal person would. All of it became fuel to make her crueler and more vicious. Better at what she did. What she did to my parents would be a good example. It wasn't that she didn't love my father. She did. But she let his betrayal—or what she saw as a betrayal—forge her into something harder."

Barnabas felt a chill as he looked at Tafa. She had been very young when her parents were taken away from her, and they had been tortured for years before they were finally executed. Tafa had grown up knowing that if she made one wrong move, she'd suffer the same fate.

The way she spoke so matter-of-factly about the event was jarring in the extreme.

"So you don't think Koel will let this stop him?" Barnabas asked slowly.

"No. He won't. He'll find a way to make an example of you if he can, and then he'll be even more powerful because everyone will be even more afraid of him." Her voice changed, and she shuddered. "Don't do this. Run and hide. He's stronger than you are."

Barnabas and Shinigami exchanged looks. Tafa had always been very calm and collected, and remarkably courageous when they considered what she had been through. Death didn't seem to scare her very much.

But this was her oldest and deepest fear, and when she spoke of it, she sounded like the child she had been when her parents were taken from her—helpless and afraid.

"Tafa, do you want to leave?" Barnabas kept his voice gentle. "There are many, many safe places we can get you to; places that aren't associated with us. Koel would never find you, and you could start a good life—"

"That's not what I'm saying!" She wiped the tears welling in her eyes. She seemed furious at her own emotion. "I'm saying you aren't invincible. I don't want you to get *hurt.*" She looked at Shinigami and Barnabas. "I don't want you to die...or worse. Shinigami, tell him the odds. You have to have some calculation for this. You've seen Koel's fleet, so you know you can't win this."

Shinigami said nothing.

Barnabas felt a heavy weight settle in his chest. "Shinigami?"

"It's not important," Shinigami replied finally.

The words were like a blow. Barnabas looked at her. "It *is* important. What are the odds? Do we have any chance of winning this?"

"Of course, we have a chance," she declared too quickly. "There's always a *chance.*"

There was a silence.

"I don't have to tell you the odds," Shinigami continued finally. "You know them."

Barnabas stood up and paced to the window. "And I'm dragging all of you into this, too. If there was a chance of success—a real one, Shinigami—I could justify it, but without one... You'll have to go."

"Who has to go?" Gar looked around the room, taking in Shinigami's silence and Tafa's tears. It wasn't entirely surprising that he came to the wrong conclusion. "Why should Tafa have to leave?"

"You all have to leave," Barnabas said not looking around.

"*All* of us?" Shinigami demanded.

"Yes." Barnabas looked her avatar in the eyes. "We'll

NATALIE GREY & MICHAEL ANDERLE

leave the AI core with Bethany Anne, and one of the EIs can pilot it."

"Bringing your odds of succeeding to pretty much zero! Speaking of which, what would even be your *plan* in that case?" She sounded furious now.

"Pretty much the same as it is now," Barnabas retorted, his voice hard. "Try to find a way to lure Koel someplace secluded and do my best to assassinate him. Without him, the Yennai Corporation should fall apart. They'd be easier for someone else to pick off. Tabitha, maybe."

Shinigami said nothing for a long moment, but when she spoke her voice was ugly. Baba Yaga echoed in her words.

"You'll die."

"That was always going to happen sometime." Barnabas smiled tightly.

To his surprise, the rest of the crew stared back at him, their expressions ranging between sadness and absolute fury.

"What?" He felt himself growing angry as well. "What do you want from me? I am doing the best I can to make sure none of you suffer for this vendetta I've apparently created. I will do what I can to end it, and the rest of you can—"

"What?" Shinigami spat. "Live the rest of our lives knowing we abandoned you when you needed us most?"

Barnabas stopped short.

"Did it ever occur to you, *genius*," Shinigami's voice was clipped, hardly human anymore now that she was so angry, "that maybe our biggest concern isn't whether *we* survive, it's what happens to our *friend*?"

For a moment, Barnabas could not speak. He turned back to the window and crossed his arms over his chest, swallowing as he looked out at the black. To his surprise, he was blinking a bit more than normal. There must be something in the air.

"That's what's bothering you all?" He was unable to face them.

"*Yes.*" The three of them spoke in unison.

"I don't get it." Gar shook his head. "You could free that mining camp in your sleep, and you still had a backup. You probably could have done the whole thing at the base yourself, too. And now, when you might actually need us—"

"When you might be in real danger, you mean." Barnabas swung around to look at him. "Gar, you've only been in a few fights. This is an entire fleet. Shinigami, you have years left. Centuries. Tafa, you've only just gotten the freedom to *live*. Why are all of you so eager to rush into danger?"

"Why are you?" Gar countered.

"Because it's the right thing to do!" Barnabas felt his hands clench. "This bastard wants to rule the universe and make it his playground. He has no excuse. He has no morals. He doesn't even pretend to value life or goodness or even the people he loves. All of it is just fuel for his ambition. There's no limit to the number of people he could hurt. I have to try to stop him; honor demands no less. And since he wants to kill me in particular…"

They looked at one another.

"We're not leaving," Shinigami asserted. "And you'd better fucking apologize for thinking we would."

NATALIE GREY & MICHAEL ANDERLE

Barnabas stared at them, his mouth opening and closing a few times.

"We have fish that do that on Luvendan," Gar commented.

Tafa gave a snort of laughter.

Before Barnabas could make any retort, there was the sound of an incoming call. He sighed as he opened it, then frowned at the screen.

"Jeltor?"

"I am *not* Jeltor." The Jotun sounded deeply aggrieved. "For one thing, Jeltor is a male."

Barnabas bit his lip to keep from asking how in the world he was supposed to know he wasn't looking at a male Jotun. As far as he could tell, this one was identical to Jeltor in every way.

However, several centuries of life had given him the skills to politely bullshit his way out of most social situations.

"My apologies," he offered smoothly. "We saw only the location. I'm sure the picture will clear up shortly. To whom do I have the pleasure of speaking, and how may I help you?"

"Hmph." She sounded mollified. "I am Commander Jeqwar of the Jotun Navy, and I have an offer for you."

"You might want to be careful with that," Barnabas cautioned. "The last person who helped me got hauled up on treason charges."

"I'm aware of that," she retorted. Her voice was tart. "We're offering anyway."

"Who's 'we?'"

"The Jotun Navy." She bobbed slightly in her tank, and

he thought he detected some smugness. It was always nice to make an offer that caused people's jaws to drop.

"The...entire navy? Are you allowed to do that?" Barnabas asked blankly.

"Who fucking cares?" The answer was sharp. "They sold us up the river. We're going to do what's right, and damn whoever tries to stop us."

Barnabas smiled. "Well, then. I'm very glad to have you on board, Admiral. I'll admit..." He looked at the rest of them and nodded to each, "that we could really use some backup on this one."

8

_____

"This is as good a system as any," Barnabas announced a few hours later. He frowned at one of the displays. "It's out of the way of...everything. No shipping lanes, no private interests, and no colonies that *anyone* knows of."

"Judging by the state of that planet, I'd certainly *hope* no one lives there." Commander Jeqwar sounded amused.

It was easy to see what she meant. The planet was so inhospitable and in such an out-of-the-way system that it was only known as 1027.478B. The atmosphere had somehow managed to trap heat while blocking absolutely none of the deadly radiation from the system's star, which was unstable and spat large plumes of gas at random intervals.

No one in their right mind would go there, which made it a perfect place for Barnabas' showdown with Koel.

The only question was how to lure him there? Barnabas and the Jotun naval officers had been planning for several hours now, and no one seemed to have any ideas. Koel was unlikely to let them dictate the terms of the battle.

"I'm going to shift processing for a bit," Shinigami told Barnabas. He looked up at her and frowned distractedly, so she made the statement a bit more human. "I'm going to step out for a few. Call if you need me."

"Oh. Right." He nodded in a way that told her he hadn't really heard anything she'd said. He was still thinking about Koel.

That suited her just fine. She had plenty to do. She had her avatar walk over to the doors, used the ship's internal controls to open them, and headed into the hallway.

If she were honest with herself, Shinigami had to admit that she enjoyed having an avatar. She didn't *need* to walk from place to place if she didn't want to, but she liked the process of learning to walk without anyone looking at her oddly. Human movement had almost endless subtleties.

She counted it as a victory every time one of the other crew members passed her in a hallway and nodded distractedly, seeing her as simply another crewmate. The other day Gar had even turned his shoulder so he wouldn't bump into her.

Gradually, the crew had become used to her presence in her almost-physical form, and she liked it. She played around with the clothes she had seen Bethany Anne wear, styled her hair however she felt like it—she didn't have to worry about gravity or humidity, after all—and tried different looks, expressions, and mannerisms from holorecordings of people she knew.

She was getting good at it.

She stuck her head around the door to Tafa's room, maintaining her projection in the corridor. "Got a second? I could use an artist's eye."

"Sure, just a moment." Tafa put down her paint brushes with relief and began cleaning them.

Tafa's painting hadn't gone well lately. When Barnabas had first brought her on board she'd painted from stress, and after that, she had painted memories and any little thing that popped into her head. Dozens of canvases leaned against the walls.

The problem was, now that Tafa had all the time in the universe to paint and could make her name as a famous artist...

The thought of picking up a paintbrush terrified her.

She made herself do it, of course, but she couldn't tell if the things she painted were any good. She had never dared sell her work, knowing that anything that made her famous would probably make Mustafee furious.

What if she wasn't good enough?

She washed her hands and followed Shinigami to the ridiculously clean conference room that had become known as Shinigami's office. This space showed the limitations of Shinigami's form more clearly than anything else. While any species gradually accumulated clutter, things they had carried into the room and forgotten, like cold cups of coffee to notepads or sweatshirts, Shinigami was incapable of doing so.

She didn't really need an office, of course, but with the ship only fractionally occupied, everyone had as much room as they wanted to spread out.

In the office, Shinigami gestured to the only chair. "Please, sit."

Tafa sat, looking curious.

"I'm working on a project." Shinigami gestured to the

screens on the side walls and they lit up, showing information in a way that would be easy for Tafa to read with her side-set eyes.

The Yofu gave Shinigami a grateful smile. "Thanks. Most people don't remember that part. You get used to looking at things on front screens, but it's a relief to be able to see things properly."

Shinigami smiled.

"What is all this, anyway?" Tafa asked.

Shinigami didn't answer. She worked on one of Barnabas' poses, leaning against the back wall with her arms crossed over her chest and one foot tucked behind the other, and she watched as Tafa read.

When Tafa was finished and looking at Shinigami again, the AI pushed her avatar off the wall—she was still working on that mannerism—and gestured at the screens.

"Of the things you saw there, what didn't seem to fit?"

This was her pet project, her only secret from Barnabas, and it was absolutely essential that it should be perfect.

In fact, though Shinigami didn't tell Tafa this, it was a matter of life and death.

Tafa considered Shinigami's question carefully. She looked at all the information and images displayed, and finally, she pointed to three pictures.

"Those."

Shinigami nodded. "Any of the facts? The writing?"

Tafa frowned. "I really don't know enough about—"

"You have an eye for the whole," Shinigami interrupted. "You can see things other people can't. Some pieces of this, like the photos, might not fit. Does anything stick out to you?"

Tafa hesitated. She was less sure this time, but she highlighted several facts.

Shinigami heaved a sigh and chewed her lip, another mannerism she had picked up from Barnabas. Tafa had, unerringly, picked several lies in the presentation. And what Tafa noticed, someone else might notice on a subliminal level.

Shinigami couldn't have that.

"Thank you. I'll call you back to look at it again when I've made some revisions."

"What is this for?" Tafa looked confused. "Shouldn't Barnabas be helping you with this?"

"Barnabas...told me to take care of it." Shinigami evaded the question with a sense of unease. Barnabas didn't know exactly what she was doing.

She was sure he would approve, though.

She walked with Tafa back to the studio, then appeared in the conference room. From the frustrated expression on Barnabas' face, little progress had been made.

But something had occurred to her as she walked.

"What if we dropped hints and scattered bits of information that sort of suggested there was a human colony being built in this sector?"

Everyone turned to look at her. Barnabas' eyebrows lifted, and the Jotuns... Well, Shinigami couldn't actually tell which direction the Jotuns looked, but they seemed to be paying attention.

"We could do that," Barnabas drawled slowly. "Something like High Tortuga. Protected, and very secretive."

"Like you said earlier," Shinigami pointed out, "we can't just leak some memo about where you'll be. He'll know that's a trap. But then it occurred to me—we know he's paid highly for information in the past. Putting things together and making plans is how he likes to work. If he thinks he's discovered something we don't want him to know…"

Which was pretty much the outline of her pet project as well. She shoved the thought away and smiled at Barnabas, hoping she didn't look guilty.

He wasn't really paying attention, though.

"What information would we need to plant?" he murmured. "Sightings of our ships. Buying materials? No, we always use our own materials."

"He's very sensitive to any distortions in trade," Commander Jeqwar noted. "It wouldn't have to be anything like buying materials. You could simply start to seed information—just rumors, whispers, nothing directly traceable—that shipping routes in a certain area were being disturbed. Say the ships had been offered money to change routes, for instance, and for not talking about it. No one would confirm it when he went digging, which would fit."

"And he'd go looking for things in that area," Shinigami continued. She grinned. "And what if we did the old trick of making a planet seem like something it wasn't…but with another layer?"

Barnabas frowned at her. "Explain."

"When someone wants a planet for themselves they try to change all the data, right? So when people look it up, they think it's a piece-of-crap planet they'd never want to go to?" Not that she'd know *anything* about doing that.

"Yes." His eyes drifted toward the Jotun officers on the screen, as if trying to see what they thought of this.

It was impossible to tell, however, given their jellyfish not-faces.

She might as well keep going.

"So we do that twice over," Shinigami explained. "First we change the data on some random planet that he's had no interest in before. Now it looks like a lovely, habitable planet—or at least, open to terraforming or enclosed colonies or something. *Then* we write over the data just a little more sloppily, making it seem like we tried to hide the fact that we can use it."

"Ah," Barnabas murmured. He was smiling now. "I do like that."

"It's clever," one of the officers agreed. "But what if he sees through it?"

"He might see through anything," Barnabas countered. "Our best shot is indeed to give him the illusion that he's seen through our attempts to hide information. That he's figured out something we wanted to keep hidden."

"At the same time, you should send him a direct challenge," Shinigami told Barnabas. "Throw down the gauntlet, tell him to meet you somewhere. Somewhere far, *far* from where the action is supposedly happening. You can't just drop off the radar after your challenge or he'll know something's up, so you pretend like you're playing it straight and then give him this secret target."

"We should..." Barnabas sighed. "We should pretend that there are a large number of civilians on that hidden colony. That will make him think he can get us by the balls."

"I'm sorry," Commander Jeqwar piped up after a moment. "I don't think that last sentence translated properly."

Shinigami snorted, and Barnabas flushed.

"I, er…I apologize. It's a way of saying that he'll think that's a place to hit us where we're weak."

"Huh." Commander Jeqwar put that down for further study. "Is this our plan, then?"

"I think so. You'll need to cover your tracks about where the Jotun fleet is," Barnabas told her. "We'll tell you when we've selected a place, and you can even reinforce the data we're planting in your systems."

"Why?"

Barnabas and Shinigami exchanged a look.

"Because Koel is almost certainly in your government databases," Shinigami told her bluntly. "That will be one of the things he bribed people to get access to."

"Oh, gods." Jeqwar let loose with a stream of words that didn't translate but didn't really need to. "We'll do what we have to do, including finding out who gave him that access." Her tone made it very clear what was going to happen to those people.

"We'll be in touch," Barnabas told her. He signed off and looked at Shinigami. "Where did you get off to?"

"Researching planets." It wasn't a lie.

"Any suggestions for your plan, then?"

She dug hastily through her data banks. "Not 1027.478B. That one is pretty well known, and none of the shipping lanes go near it. He might have that as ambient knowledge. I'd suggest Waler's Star. One of the planets there is *just* too inhospitable for any colonies to take root. If we make it seem like we have the technology and want to make sure no one tries to take it first…"

"I'll trust your judgment." Barnabas nodded decisively. "Let's get started, then."

9

O n the bridge of the *Avaris*, Lotar Venn frowned at the screen and punched a few keys. What he saw in the data couldn't possibly be correct...could it? And it might be nothing, anyway. He had to be very, very sure of what he suspected before he brought anything to the admiral—and to Mr. Yennai.

Lotar gulped. Koel Yennai was a legend. People said that when they made reports to him his face never changed. That it was impossible to know what he thought until you stopped talking and he began to ask questions.

And if you didn't have answers...

That was a fast track to ruining your entire career. When Lotar had first been brought onboard the *Avaris*, everyone had hastened to assure him that he shouldn't worry that he'd be *executed* for something like that. No, not for something like that.

He'd found that to be the opposite of reassuring.

"What *did* happen?" he had asked them finally, and they all looked at one another meaningfully. Your career was definitely finished if you wasted Mr. Yennai's time. You got shuffled off…somewhere; no one knew exactly where. It wasn't anywhere you wanted to go, though. One or two of them shared stories about bunkmates who'd committed that grave offense and managers and company officers who had failed to do their due diligence.

Anyway, you had to be sure, they said. That was the point. Just be *sure*, if you were going to bring information to Mr. Yennai, that your research was unassailable and you'd drawn sound conclusions.

Lotar had consequently spent the past six months absolutely terrified of finding anything that would mean he had to present a report. Now that he had, his palms were clammy, and he wondered if he could just pass the report to his managers and let them handle it.

He'd do the research first, though. In his heart, Lotar was an academic. He loved to put together puzzles and draw pictures from scraps of information. He'd proven adept at all the tests they'd given him when he was interviewed to join the corporation—finding trade opportunities, noting market manipulation, and suggesting avenues for data collection.

Now, this was live data, and he was doing everything in real time, and he was grinning as he punched the keys.

Yes, someone had definitely manipulated data. They had tried to be clever, but he'd caught them. He added images and facts to the report. Which facts had been changed on which date? What other source might there be?

Once or twice he made emphatic points, only to go back and revise them. If he wasn't sure of something, he withheld it. He took comfort, as he always did, in the data.

The patterns were there. Data, unlike people, didn't lie. The data points were what they were.

By the time he'd finished his report, he was finally feeling relaxed and happy. He flexed his fingers, smiled to himself, and spun in his chair—

To see Koel Yennai watching him.

The bottom dropped out of Lotar's stomach. He froze, staring at the Torcellan patriarch in absolute terror.

Then Koel smiled. "I watched you build the report," he admitted. His voice was melodious. No one had ever mentioned that about him. "It's a good one. You've drawn very reasonable conclusions, with a good balance between unfounded speculation, and over-caution. What is your name?"

Lotar managed to close his mouth, but his mind was still a complete blank.

What *was* his name? He only just managed to avoid looking at the nameplate on his desk.

"Lotar Venn, Mr. Yennai."

"Lotar Venn." Koel smiled, which transformed his face. For a moment, Lotar felt like he was the only person in the universe. "I am pleased to have you as one of my employees. Forward that report directly to me."

"But it's not... I mean, of course, sir." Lotar swallowed. "But I don't have a final conclusion yet. I mean, I don't know who's doing this. It's someone who has the technology to terraform a planet that no one else has been able to, and I have no idea who's made an advance like that recently."

Koel smiled again, and this time the smile was chilling.

"I believe I know just who is doing this. They've been spreading like a virus through many systems."

Lotar's eyes were wide. "Who are they? The Jotuns?"

"They're part of it." There was a distant rage in Koel's eyes. "But the main instigators are a race called 'humans.' And now that we know where one of their colonies is..." He gave another cold smile. "We can make sure they understand the consequences of taking what is not theirs."

He swept away, and Lotar stared after him. With shaking fingers, he sent the report.

He no longer wanted to, but he had to. What was about to happen to this colony was the inevitable result of angering Koel Yennai.

Lotar wasn't brave enough to risk that himself.

Zinqued was whistling as he headed for the airlock. The *Julentai* had just docked at Virtue Station, and he was certain that he'd find more talent for his crew here.

Then he stopped in the door of the airlock, frowning.

Tik'ta was slumped against one wall, her shoulders hunched. She looked like she was trying not to throw up. When the automated alert let them know that docking was nearly complete, the look of nausea on her face only got more intense.

"Are you all right?" Zinqued asked her cautiously.

"I…will be."

"Are you sick?" He hung back. If she *were* sick, he'd have Chofal take care of her. In a crew with multiple species, it was best to make sure that diseases didn't have a good vector.

She gave a tired smile. "No, not like that. It's just, now that we're here... I remember what happened the last time I was here."

Zinqued realized what she must mean. "You never came back after the first time you encountered the *Shinigami*?"

"No." She shook her head. "Why would we? Nothing legitimate goes on here, and he told us we had to be doing legitimate things, and..." She closed her eyes. "Klafk'tin was an ass. Why do I care that he got killed? He deserved it."

Zinqued remembered the sea of dead bodies he'd seen in the Yennai Corporation headquarters. "I know what you mean, though. This guy is dangerous." He smiled at Tik'ta as he stepped into the airlock and let it close behind him. "So's the Yennai Corporation. That's why we're letting them battle to the death while we come in and pick up the stuff they leave behind."

She looked a little brighter at that. "That's a good point. It's a smart plan. We don't have to pick a side, we just have to swoop in and get all the things they won't be using anymore once they're dead."

"Exactly," Zinqued agreed.

The alert announced that decontamination was complete, and the airlock opened into Virtue Station's docking bay.

"Should I keep the ship warmed up?" Chofal asked over the channel.

"There shouldn't be any need," Zinqued told her. "Just stay put and be ready to run background checks on any names I give you. I'll want to hire them immediately if I can."

"I'll be ready."

Zinqued and Tik'ta forged their way into the docking bay. To Zinqued's surprise, it was incredibly busy—and most of the people seemed to have suitcases and packing crates.

"What the hell is going on?" he asked Tik'ta in an undertone.

"I don't know."

"They're leaving," Chofal reported. "The transports out are booked for the next week, and more transports are being called in. There are whispers that the Yennai Corporation is about to fall apart, and since they basically run this place…"

Zinqued whistled and shook his head.

People could be so stupid sometimes. After all, when something like the Yennai Corporation failed, there was chaos and a power vacuum—and that was the best time to turn a profit.

He shouldn't complain, though. The more people who decided to run, the fewer people he'd be competing with to find new employees.

And now that he knew there was a panic, he was prepared to be bolder.

"Let's go to the main level."

"Us?" She looked down at her coveralls. "They'll never let us into any of the banks."

"We don't need to go *in*," Zinqued said. "Not exactly. You'll see when we get there."

Koel Yennai sat back in his desk chair and smiled. The new employee had done well. Koel had seen him a few times and had been told that he was expected to do good work, but in the chaos of the past few months, there hadn't been much time for business as usual.

It turned out they'd been correct about him, though. Lotar Venn had found something very impressive indeed.

A small planet in orbit around Waler's Star was being adapted for human settlement. There wasn't much in the way of direct detail, just rumors and whispers. Lotar had successfully seen through all of it, though.

Koel was reminded of himself when he was younger. He'd always been able to see patterns no one else could.

And now he would put that skill to use, as he had so many times before, to stop his enemies in their tracks. When the humans saw the wreckage of their colony and thousands of their civilians dead...

They would break and run.

He opened a channel to the bridge. "Admiral Frist."

"Yes, Mr. Yennai?"

"I'm sending you coordinates," Koel told him. "Begin moving the fleet immediately."

The Brakalon at the door of the main bank was one of the biggest aliens Zinqued had ever seen. His skin was a deep bluish-green, and his eyes never stopped moving. He looked endlessly suspicious, not relaxing his vigilance even for the rich clients who swept past him in their jewels and expensive clothes. He seemed to hate them.

He was perfect.

Zinqued approached him, catching his eye and nodding decisively.

"What do you want?" the Brakalon called, not sounding friendly in the least.

"To offer you a job." Zinqued stopped a few feet away. "You have time to talk?"

"I'm on the job." The Brakalon scoffed. But he looked inside the bank, where the rich clients were all shrieking that they needed their money at once, and his lip curled. He headed over to Zinqued a moment later. "Fucking idiots, the lot of them."

"There's going to be a lot up for grabs if the Yennai Corporation falls apart," Zinqued observed. "A lot of rich people abandoning a lot of property. A lot of places where anything we want could be ours. Of course, we'd need some good talent in case other people had the same idea."

The Brakalon started to smile. He nodded.

"Yeah. You would. You'd need someone who could fight." He looked at Tik'ta. "Doesn't look like she can."

"Damned good pilot, though," Zinqued replied equably. "And the best engineer I've seen. You'd be the fourth—you and anyone else you'd recommend."

The Brakalon thought this over, then smiled. "Yeah, I think I know some people. I'd get a cut for bringing them on, right?"

"Of course." Zinqued shook his hand and tried not to wince at the Brakalon's bone-crushing grip. "Meet us at Bay 27. One hour."

"Will do." The guard stepped back, talking into his communications unit in a low voice, and Zinqued turned to Tik'ta with a smile.

"And we have some fighters."

She grinned at him. "Good. Because he's right, I'm not one for the front lines."

"And I'd guess he can't fly the ship," Zinqued added with a laugh. "Doubt he could fit in the cockpit. We're getting a good team together. We have a good shot at this."

otar Venn had just about managed to recover from his last meeting with Koel Yennai when he was summoned to the patriarch's staterooms.

"I don't think I can go," he told Era, his closest friend on the ship.

"You want to get thrown out an airlock?" She gave him a look, then rolled her eyes at his expression. "I'm *kidding*. God, you'd think you'd never been part of an organization with a trigger-happy megalomaniac at the helm."

Lotar looked around nervously to see if anyone else was listening.

No one seemed to care.

"It makes me nervous when you talk like that."

"*Everything* makes you nervous." She flipped over a tile in her game and rolled her eyes again. "Go away, Venn. He's moving the fleet, nothing's stopped. He probably wants to promote you."

"That—"

"Makes you nervous. Yes. We all know. Go away before someone punches you."

Lotar left and considered it a win that she'd said it instead of just punching him without giving a heads up first.

Koel waited by a window that took up one whole wall of the apartment. It was so clear that Lotar had a feeling of vertigo. Staring into the black, it wasn't like there were references that would show how big it was.

But you *knew*. You knew when you looked at it.

He gulped, said a quick prayer, and walked over to where Koel stood with his hands linked behind his back, staring at the fleet.

"Mr. Yennai." Lotar ducked his head as far as he could without making it a bow. He didn't want to be a kiss-ass, but he didn't want to piss Koel off either.

Koel's pale, cold features were arranged in a smile. He seemed deeply pleased with the state of things.

"What do you think of the fleet?" he asked.

"It's a very nice fleet," Lotar said automatically. Then his brain caught up with him, and he flushed. "I mean, ah, it's nicely balanced. And these ships are the most advanced of any out there."

Koel gave a wry smile. "Perhaps."

"It could defeat any other fleet," Lotar insisted.

"I hope it will never have to," Koel told him. He went to one of the couches and sat, gesturing for Lotar to join him. "Do you know, I have read the great philosophers and military strategists of every species, and they all say the same thing. To defeat an enemy on the field of battle means you have already failed. It is better to have your enemy surrender to you before your armies ever meet."

Lotar had never thought of that before. He perched on the edge of a couch and tried not to look too out of place.

"But if you never use your army..." His voice trailed off, and he flushed. "My apologies, sir. I am clearly not a military strategist."

"Not yet," Koel agreed. He picked up a tablet from the table beside him. "This tablet has the books I mentioned. I want you to read them, and then I want to discuss them with you."

Lotar took the tablet with wide eyes. "I... With me? Why?"

"I see much of myself in you," he declared finally as he surveyed the fleet. "The Yennai Corporation needs a future, Mr. Venn. Perhaps you will be that future. Who can say?"

Lotar could not speak, he was so shocked. He hugged the tablet to his chest and ducked his head. "Thank you, Mr. Yennai."

"Now, come with me to see the pride of my fleet." Koel stood and gestured for Lotar to follow him to the window.

He pointed to a strange, almost hollow-looking ship. "You see her? She is one of my greatest achievements."

Lotar studied the ship. "Where are its weapons?"

"You mean missiles, but it has none." Koel smiled confidently. "Nonetheless, that ship will be our victory, Mr. Venn. The schematics are also in your tablet, as is an inventory of the ship's contents. Return tomorrow to tell me what you think."

"Yes, Mr. Yennai."

NATALIE GREY & MICHAEL ANDERLE

"The Yennai fleet is moving," Shinigami reported. She had watched the communications of the fleet for days before the order had been sent. "Should I relay word to the Jotun high command?"

Barnabas looked up from his book. "Use the personal channel Commander Jeqwar gave," he instructed. "We're still not sure where Koel has bugs in the Jotuns' systems—unless they've gotten back to you on that."

"Not yet." Shinigami's avatar flickered into being. She sat at the pilot's chair and positioned her hands over the controls, moving them as the ship began to turn.

"A good illusion." Barnabas smiled. "If I didn't know better, I'd say you were flying the ship with those gestures, not from inside the computers."

"I could do it, too, if you would give me a body."

"For one thing, you'd need to pick a look and stick with it," Barnabas said, amused. "For another…no. You don't get a robotic body. That's just asking for trouble."

"ADAM is getting one!"

"Not yet. And I think it will be a mistake if he does. For one thing, you'd be pestering me to come on combat missions if you got a body."

Shinigami had to work hard not to smile. She didn't want to let Barnabas see her satisfaction, because that would put him on his guard. But the fact was, in a few short weeks, she'd gotten him from a simple "no" to debating the idea on its own merits.

And she really, really wanted her own body. She got to

walk around the ship, but that was nothing compared to seeing all the places Barnabas went.

When she looked through his eyes, it just wasn't the same.

She was determined to get him to agree to it. For now, she dropped the subject with a smile and went back to Koel. They could bond over how much they hated him.

"So this motherfucker thinks he's going after an undefended colony full of innocent bystanders, huh?"

Barnabas' face went absolutely cold. "Yes. He does. And we are going to make sure he learns how much of a mistake that was."

Shinigami tried to swivel in the chair, cursed internally when the chair didn't move, and flickered over to the other side of the room to make her avatar lean against the wall.

"What if he finds out about the Jotun fleet in advance?"

"Then we'll know there's a spy in their high command," Barnabas replied. "He may have advance notice, which would not be optimal, but regardless, he'll have an entire fleet to face down." He frowned. "I hope the Jotun fleet knows what they're doing. They're confident, but…"

"Their track record suggests they're good at small-scale engagements, at least." Shinigami brought up a few reports on the displays. She had spent considerable time verifying the capabilities of the fleet.

She didn't want to die, after all.

Barnabas looked them over with his arms crossed. "They really took to technology, I'll give them that. *How*, I have no idea. They're aquatic. How did they learn electronics without killing themselves?"

Shinigami snickered. "Maybe they started millennia ago

and lost thousands in the process." She shrugged. "My guess is that they appropriated some technology and made some allies, and it all took off from there. You have to give them credit, though. Those ships are insane."

"How do you mean?" He frowned.

"You didn't see how they're controlled?" Shinigami hopped up on one of the control panels to sit cross-legged.

"One of the things you can't do in a robotic body," Barnabas remarked.

"Yeah, yeah. Maybe I'll just park my body when we come back to the ship and use my avatar."

"Leaving the robotic body to stand like a creepy mannequin in the hallway? I think not."

"That is *such* a good idea."

"No. No, it's not. Don't do that." Barnabas' expression was vaguely panicked.

Shinigami gave him a toothy grin. "*Anyway.* The Jotun ships. They're controlled telekinetically. Sort of. That's the closest word for it."

"You'd mentioned that. I thought it was that the power-suits were telekinetic and—"

"Oh, no. That's not how it works." Shinigami brought up some pictures on the display. "You see this? This is Admiral Jutfa. Well, theoretically it is, but they could put a Jotun stuffed animal in there and none of us would be able to tell the difference."

Barnabas sank his head into his hands with a groan. "I can never tell who's calling when I answer the call, and they always expect me to *know*. How am I supposed to tell them apart?"

"Fuck if I know." Shinigami shook her head. "Anyway,

you see the admiral isn't wearing a normal powersuit, right? Well, when they go into battle, they plug the captain of the ship *into the ship* and they control the whole thing—weapons, maneuvering, all of it. In extreme cases, they can network the tasks and put other people in control, but mostly, the captain just controls all of that at once. They communicate with the officers and operate based on that information."

Barnabas stared at her with his mouth hanging open. "That's not possible."

"Oh, but it is." Shinigami gave him a look that said, *I'm as surprised as you are.* "Believe me, I didn't just take all that for granted. I checked."

"Holy shit," Barnabas muttered, then flushed. "My vocabulary has gone over a cliff since I started associating with Tabitha."

"It's good for you." Shinigami believed strongly that Barnabas needed to unwind a little. Unfortunately, it was almost impossible to get him drunk. "And 'holy shit' is about the size of it. People get promoted in the Jotun Navy because they can manage a ship that big. An admiral can manage multiple ships at once."

Barnabas was frowning now. "I'm a little worried that we've underestimated the Jotuns."

"It's possible, but as far as I can tell they just have really good multitasking abilities. Let's not panic." Shinigami shrugged. "After all, Jeltor is a nice guy. Perfectly smart, but not an evil genius by any means."

"Still." Barnabas chewed his lip. "All right. Let's get Gar and Tafa and tell them the drill. I think I have an idea what Koel is going to do when he sees us there with the fleet."

11

"Don't you want me to stand still?" Gar questioned. He stood frozen in the act of putting on his armor. His weapons lay neatly to one side, cleaned after their last battle but not yet checked this time.

Barnabas was methodical to a fault, and he expected the same of Gar.

"No," Tafa said impatiently. "The painting isn't of *you*, it's of… Well, *you*."

"You can see how I'd get confused," Gar joked.

"It isn't your face or your shape." Tafa gestured to him. "It's of your…what do Luvendi call it? Your essence? All the thoughts and energy that make you who you are."

"Thoughts and energy?" Gar considered. "I think humans call it a soul. It's their closest concept, anyway. Not exactly the same thing. Thoughts are the mind. Energy is… energy. Emotions. The soul is… Now I'm confused."

"The riddle," Barnabas said, poking his head in the door as he went past, "is that if I have a mind and a body and a soul…what am I?" He smiled and disappeared again.

"I'm going to make a painting about that," Tafa said slowly.

"I'm going to get a headache thinking about it," Gar added.

"Anyway, the point is, keep moving around. I need to see you move to paint you." Tafa spread a dollop of red paint on her palette.

"I'm red?" Gar looked dubious. "I'm from Luvendan. Everything is blue. My eyes are blue. My skin is kind of blue."

"Well, your essence is red," Tafa stated emphatically. "Trust me."

"Sure, why not?" Gar adjusted the thin layer that went under his armor and moved on to inspecting his weapons. He disassembled a pistol carefully, checking each piece for grime.

"You are afraid before battles," Tafa commented.

"I am not." Gar looked up at once, offended. "I'm glad to go into battle. I'm fighting for what's right."

"Those aren't mutually exclusive." She swooped the brush across one of the canvases and made a slash on the other, wielding both brushes with precision despite the quick movements. "Gar, your whole life, you've feared physical contact. It could damage you. So much of who you are is tied up in being the person who was…fragile. Every time you dealt with someone, both of you knew that you could be beaten to a pulp within minutes. That doesn't go away in a few months."

Gar sighed in exasperation, his hands still on the pistol. Having fewer fingers than a human, he had to concentrate to get the gun to come apart correctly, and Tafa was ruining his focus.

"Maybe right before a battle isn't the best time for this."

"When *would* be a good time?" When he said nothing, Tafa nodded. "Exactly. You don't want to confront it. When you fight, you're not fighting because it's the right thing to do, you're fighting because you want to show all those people who underestimated you that they were wrong."

"You make it sound like I don't care about what's right!"

"When you're in a battle, you don't—not from what I've seen." She sat next to him. "Gar, you follow Barnabas because you want to do the right thing. I know that. But when it comes time for a battle, you just want to surprise them; make them pay for underestimating you. You know...you know there's no shame in being what you were before, right?"

Gar looked down at the guns. He heard the blood pounding in his ears.

"What I was before," he said precisely, "was nothing. I was useless."

"Not true." Tafa shook her head. "If that were true, Barnabas would never have enhanced your abilities.

"Barnabas fights from his heart, Gar. His abilities...they aren't *him.* He could be in that body with the strong bones and the speed and all of it, and he still wouldn't be able to do what he does without his *belief.* That's why he chose you. Because you have that, too. Not because he thought you'd hit the hardest when he upgraded your body."

Gar realized he was shaking. Ever since he'd left Luvendan he'd been the weak one; the fragile one. Everyone he'd met looked him up and down with contempt. In his work he'd held the uneasy position at the top of the ladder, ordering people around who could have easily killed him—and had often wanted to.

Leaving that physical weakness behind had been everything he wanted. And yet…

"I'm more afraid now than I was when I was weak." The sentiment made no sense, but it was true.

Tafa nodded. "That's what the red is. It's fear. You fear and hate weakness because you believed it defined you. But it never did, Gar. You could be what Barnabas is, but until you accept what you were, you never will."

He said nothing, and she moved toward the door to give him some privacy.

"What *is* Barnabas?" Gar called after her. "You say I can be what he is, but what is that, to you?"

Tafa paused. "I've been reading about Earth. In their stories, they talk about knights, people who swore on their honor to defend the helpless. But there's a kind of warrior who's even more than that—a paladin."

Gar frowned. He'd never heard that term before.

"They're a myth," Tafa explained. "Sort of. I think. They draw their power from a deity and wield it like magic." She paused. "But Barnabas…I think what he draws his power from is the very concept of goodness, itself. Evil is *evil* because it hurts the innocent. Good is *good* because it saves them. That is who he is. That is who you could be, Gar."

She left Gar to his thoughts.

Shinigami had been listening, and her avatar wore a speculative expression.

Barnabas looked up from his schematics and caught

sight of it. His brow furrowed. "What are you thinking about?"

"Not important." She wasn't sure what she thought of Tafa's theory yet—and anyway, he'd be embarrassed to hear it.

Although she wouldn't mind embarrassing him.

She'd keep that in the bank then, to use when she most needed to catch him off-guard. With a grin, Shinigami stood her avatar up and walked over to stare down at the schematics.

She had found that acting like a human—having the mannerisms that showed she was paying attention—helped her interact with the crew. When they saw expressions and actions, they let their guard down in a different way.

Barnabas looked over the known specifications for the *Avaris*, Koel Yennai's flagship. Some informants speculated he might even be aboard the ship, which Shinigami privately considered to be likely. Koel hadn't lived at the secret base, after all, and while he might have an even more top-secret base, she guessed that he was the sort of person who couldn't stay cooped up.

"No one has ever met their fleet in battle," Barnabas said worriedly. "They could have weapons we've never encountered. Even the Jotuns, who *have seen* some of their ships, don't have any idea—and Yennai knows what the Jotuns have. They've been all through that information."

He rubbed his forehead wearily.

"Having good weapons isn't the same as knowing how to use them," Shinigami pointed out. "It's like handing a four-year-old a chess board. You can tell them what each piece does. They might even understand it. That doesn't mean they can win." She smiled mischievously. "Like *you* with a chess board, now that I think of it."

Barnabas gave her a look. "You want to go? Let's go."

Shinigami gave a pointed look at the corner of the room where the stone chess board Barnabas had commissioned was sitting at a small table. "I would, but I'm incorporeal and can't pick up the pieces."

Barnabas leaned forward with his knuckles braced on the table and a wicked grin on his lips. "You're worried that if you can't cheat, you can't win," he said softly.

"I'm afraid of nothing."

"Prove it."

Shinigami narrowed her eyes. "As soon as this battle is over, old geezer, I'm going to take you down. I'll crush you so hard the whole group of Rangers won't be able to play chess for a month. I'll crush you so hard you can't *look* at a chess board. I'll crush you so hard we'll have to switch to poker."

"Poker?" Barnabas' mouth twitched. "You want to inject some random chance into our games? Bring. It. On. Chaos only benefits me."

Shinigami scoffed and narrowed her eyes. "Organic life forms are ridiculous."

Barnabas did not look at all disheartened by that. In fact, he seemed to enjoy it. "Also, I'd like to see you play chess with Tabitha. You think *I'm* infuriating? She'd break your soul. That woman is chaos personified."

Shinigami gave a shudder. She could just picture Tabitha's attempts to play chess. *What does this piece do? I don't want to move it that way. Okay, but if I could move a castle diagonally I'd have won, so technically I did win.*

"That's a horrifying thing to imagine," she confessed.

From Barnabas' smile, he planned to use this against her. "Mmmhmm." He took another look at the schematics and shook his head. "Dwelling on this isn't going to do any good. I'm going to the armory to get geared up."

"I'll come with you." Shinigami fell in beside him, and they walked through the halls in silence. Gar was alone in Tafa's studio, dressed for battle and staring out a window. He didn't seem to hear them as they passed.

Shinigami used the scanners in the room to assess him. He seemed troubled, apparently still thinking over what Tafa had said. Shinigami couldn't understand why it would trouble him. If he didn't like how he was, why wouldn't he simply change?

There was so much about organic life forms that made no sense.

She'd talk to him about it later.

She practiced her walking while Barnabas stripped off his jacket and button-down shirt and situated his armor over the thin shirt he always wore. He flexed all his joints to make sure that the armor wouldn't impede his motions. By this point, it fit like a dream. It was more habit than anything else.

He checked his weapons and brushed a few specks of grime off—imaginary grime, if Shinigami were to bet. Barnabas never left his weapons in anything but perfect condition.

He had just slid his Jean Dukes into their holsters when the call came in. It was tagged as being from Jeltor. Shinigami brought it up on the armory's screen.

"Jeltor," Barnabas said. "We're decelerating in a few minutes." He frowned. "Did you beat us there?"

Shinigami also frowned. There was no way the Jotun fleet should have beat them. The *Shinigami's* propulsion systems were state of the art, and they'd been closer to the target planet than the Jotun fleet in any case.

"It's not that." Jeltor bobbed anxiously in the tank of his powersuit. "We've just received a distress call."

"It's a trap," Barnabas declared instantly. "They know the Jotun Navy is involved. Don't get dragged off course."

"*No,*" Jeltor stated urgently. "You don't understand. The call isn't for us to come somewhere. It's… One of our ships has been captured. A civilian transport."

Barnabas frowned. "You can't go after it—"

But in a flash, Shinigami understood. She cut him off with a shake of her head. "That's not what Jeltor means. I'll bet you anything that when the Yennai Corporation fleet shows up, they'll have that civilian ship right in the middle of them so we can't shoot."

"Yes." Jeltor sounded bleak. "There are two thousand civilians on that ship. We have to call this off. We can't let them pay for—"

"We're *not* calling it off." Barnabas' voice was hard. His expression was compassionate as he looked at the screen, however. "They aren't going to die, Jeltor. He won't throw away his bargaining chip so early in the game, and there's something he wants far more than he wants the Jotuns to suffer. He wants me dead."

Shinigami sank her head into her hands. She could guess what Barnabas had planned, and it was risky—riskier than she was comfortable with.

Barnabas looked at her, raising an eyebrow. He could tell what she thought. "Do you have a better plan?" he challenged.

"No, but that's not the point."

"It's definitely the point." His fingers flexed, then clenched. "Koel Yennai is a dangerous bastard, but he's also vengeful—and that's our way in. Jeltor?"

"Yes?"

"As soon as the Yennai fleet comes in, you and I are transporting to that flagship."

12

Lotar was on the bridge of the *Avaris* when it came out of FTL.

He wasn't at his desk; it was conspicuously empty. Instead, he stood with Koel at the massive windows on the bridge. He could feel the eyes of his fellow analysts. Were they jealous?

He imagined they were, and it was a heady feeling.

He had stayed up late into the night, reading Koel's favorite books on military strategy until his eyes drooped shut. When he had woken up, he'd barely paused to put on a new uniform before presenting himself at Koel's stateroom. Lotar had plans. He had thoughts about the books he'd read, he had seen the schematics of the strange, hollow ship and its contents, and he was only too eager to talk to Koel about all of it.

His fear of Koel was entirely gone. The Torcellan was brilliant; anyone could see that. He listened to Lotar's theories and offered his own, enjoying nothing more than coming up with strategies and far-reaching plans.

When they'd received word that the fleet was coming out of FTL near Waler's Star, they had walked onto the bridge together. As Lotar made for his desk, Koel had said carelessly, "No, I'll need you with me during the battle."

Lotar was rising fast, and nothing had ever felt more satisfying in his life. Let the rest of them eat their hearts out. They'd tormented him for being the newbie and not knowing the ropes, for being too cautious, and making his reports too detailed.

Well, here he was now. He was still smiling when the fleet came out of hyperspace...

And everyone on the bridge gasped. Koel's mouth drew back in a snarl and Lotar pressed his hands against the window, mouth open in shock.

It was the Jotun fleet—and if it wasn't the whole fleet, then it was damned close.

They should have known where the fleet would be. Their sources in the Jotun senate had gleefully reported that most of the top brass were under investigation, news that had spread all through the Yennai analyst corps, and then...

Nothing. Clearly, the Jotun Navy had realized they had a leak. And now...

"Unveil the captured ship," Koel ordered.

"Yes, sir." The admiral relayed the orders.

The hollow ship slid forward from the center of the Yennai Corporation fleet, accompanied by a contingent of destroyers. Almost a sphere, the ship had a large open space in the center where mechanical arms held the civilian transport in place.

"I thought we'd only be using this against Barnabas,"

Koel said softly. "But it will work well for them, too. They'll pay for this."

Lotar said nothing. His fear of Koel rushed back.

"Sir, we're being hailed by the *Shinigami*." The admiral looked at Koel, and Lotar recognized the same fear in his eyes.

Koel turned to him slowly, then nodded for him to play the message.

"They say they are sending Barnabas and the Jotun who attacked our headquarters." The admiral tapped a few keys and highlighted a shuttle flying close to the human ship. "To speak with you, sir."

"To speak with me." Koel smiled. "Yes, send them in."

He looked at Lotar.

"The thing about Barnabas," he said quietly, "is that he doesn't really understand his limitations."

Lotar swallowed. He'd heard the stories of what happened at headquarters. He didn't think Barnabas *had* limitations, and he was suddenly afraid that Koel would get them all killed.

Koel saw his fear and his smile grew. "Barnabas expects me to want to kill him," he said. "And I do. He expects me to throw overwhelming force at him. And I will. He'll defeat them, but I have more tricks up my sleeve than just that."

"Are you sure this will work?" Jeltor asked nervously.

"Not...precisely." Barnabas cursed the ethics that kept him honest. "Let's just say I think it's a good bet.

"Bets are all we have in battle," Barnabas continued. "It's one of the reasons we don't go into battle often."

Jeltor nodded glumly at that. "All the same, if you had asked me which fleet we feared most, I would have said this one."

Barnabas nodded. The *Avaris* was so big it blotted out the stars as they approached. They continued past the hollow ship with its captive transport and Barnabas took a long look, letting Shinigami watch through his eyes.

She had to know what they were up against. As soon as the shuttle docked she would cloak the ship, leave a buoy in her place to make it seem as if she had stayed in formation with the Jotun fleet, and rescue the civilian transport.

When Barnabas had regretfully told Gar that he would have to stay on the *Shinigami*, Gar had reacted better than Barnabas had expected. He only nodded. Barnabas would have to think about that later.

Koel was going to throw everything he had at them as soon as they docked. In fact, Barnabas was surprised that the *Avaris* hadn't simply tried to shoot the shuttle out of the sky. He'd used a scrambling technique that Shinigami devised to make the shuttle show up in a slightly different location on scanners, which would buy them a few moments if they needed them.

But missiles or not, Koel definitely had something up his sleeve.

An officer with a completely expressionless voice guided them to the main landing bay, which appeared to be entirely empty.

"Get ready," Barnabas warned grimly. He looked around. "I see doors every ten meters or so, and if I had to guess, I'd say we'll be surrounded within moments of stepping from this shuttle."

"You're betting they won't kill us," Jeltor guessed.

"Yes—both because they'll be ordered not to, and because we won't let them." Barnabas looked at him. "Jeltor, being on one of your ships was also a gamble. You know that."

That at least made Jeltor relax slightly. He nodded. "Yes, I know that."

The shuttle jolted as it set down. "Good," Barnabas finished. "Because we're here."

"I'm going to regret this."

"Oh, stop being so dramatic. It's going to be fun!"

"Has anyone ever told you that humans have a very strange idea of fun?" Jeltor grumbled as they exited the shuttle. "Or is it just you?"

"It's just him," Shinigami reported, making use of the communications channel to speak to Jeltor as well. "Although really, the whole upper tier of the Etheric Empire had a few screws loose."

"One of whom you're modeled after," Barnabas ground out.

"Were we talking about me? We were not."

"We'll have to continue this another time, unfortunately." Barnabas watched as the doors opened. "We're about to have company."

The soldiers who entered the landing bay were fast and deadly. They immediately took cover, firing well-targeted shots in the direction of Barnabas and Jeltor, as well as the shuttle itself. They moved easily in their armor and shouted commands to one another.

Barnabas rolled behind the shuttle with Jeltor. He grinned at the Jotun. "Well, this is a nice surprise. It's always a treat to fight someone competent."

"You're crazy," Jeltor grumped. He ran a scan. "I make it eighteen of them. Four are up in the rafters, waiting to pick us off if we make too much trouble. You approve of that, don't you?"

"Oh, very much. It feels unsporting to kill people who don't have a fighting chance." Barnabas studied the readout on Jeltor's suit's screen. "All right, I'll take the two on the left, you take the two on the right."

They emerged, and Jeltor shot tiny missiles at the two snipers on his side. A small spread—minuscule at this range—covered a range of a few feet in either direction, and though both snipers dove, both were struck. Their bodies tumbled from the rafters and hit the floor with a thud.

Barnabas' shots left two smoking holes in the rafters. He smiled at Jeltor as they ducked back behind the shuttle, shots ringing out overhead and ricocheting off the ground nearby. "Jean has a way with weapons."

Jeltor snorted in amusement. "I hope so, because we've really pissed them off."

With a roar, the fourteen remaining soldiers hurtled over the barriers and rushed them, shooting. There was a crash, and the window of the shuttle shattered. Barnabas swore.

"They *would*. I guess we'll be finding another way out of here."

"Only you would say that," Jeltor muttered. "As if fourteen elite soldiers weren't enough to contend with."

Barnabas rolled a grenade into the mass of soldiers.

BOOM!

"There aren't fourteen of them anymore," he said cheekily. "See you on the other side. Speaking of which—swap sides with me."

He slid out and vaulted to the top of the shuttle before flipping off.

The soldiers tried to stop and turn, but they were too late—and those on this side of the shuttle had expected Jeltor. Barnabas picked off two of them before they managed to turn properly, and leaped again as the other soldiers headed toward him.

Behind him there was a roar, then a few screams.

Jeltor gets to use a flamethrower and I don't? Shinigami demanded.

Not now, Shinigami!

Barnabas dropped his shoulder and pivoted on the ball of his foot as a soldier rushed him. A shot passed harmlessly through the space where his torso had been, and a moment later his foot caught the soldier in the temple. The fighter toppled sideways, and Barnabas' shot finished him as he stumbled and fell.

Barnabas charged forward as the rest tried to regroup. They surrounded him, but hadn't planned for this and did not want to shoot one another.

Too bad. He grabbed one's rifle and pressed the finger on the trigger, dragging the soldier past him. The shot took a fellow soldier, and Barnabas' teeth ripped into the shooting soldier's throat a moment later.

They had counted on guns and knives, but not teeth.

He made short work of the rest. Two fired as he

ducked, and he shot them both in the shins and, as they fell, in the head.

The last tried to run. Barnabas caught him at the doors and sank his teeth into his neck. He threw the lifeless body to the ground.

"Jeltor?"

"All good."

Jeltor had just clanked over to him when a section of the landing bay lit up. Behind a reinforced pane of glass was the control center, and there…

"Barnabas." Koel's smooth voice came over the comm as he swept into the control center. He wore white robes which accented the pallor of his skin, and his hair was unadorned.

Barnabas' eyebrows went up at that. He had only seen mercenaries and pirates go without the traditional Torcellan hair adornments. Someone like Koel, who had all the status and money anyone could want and who certainly took care with his appearance, *should* have very ornate decorations in his hair.

Then Barnabas remembered. Koel was likely in mourning.

It was an elaborate act. Of that, Barnabas had no doubt. Koel curated his public appearance very carefully. He would not show anyone his emotions unless he believed they were useful.

Barnabas nodded sardonically. "Koel."

A figure at Koel's side stirred. It was an Ixtali.

"You will address him as Mr. Yennai," the figure said. "Or 'sir.'"

Barnabas gave a slight smile. "I think I have been extraordinarily polite, considering."

Koel laughed. He strolled closer to the window to look Barnabas in the eyes.

"I wanted to see you fight," he said. "You destroyed the headquarters, but I did not get to see what happened there. Still, I knew what you were up against. Ilia had told me how she was fortifying the place. Now I see how you got through."

Shinigami, are you close?

You mean, can I get Gar in there as a backup if you really *piss him off?*

Yes.

I'm dealing with a few contingents of fighters here...

Fine, fine.

Barnabas looked Koel in the eyes. "Uleq died well."

Koel's fingers spasmed, and he locked them behind his back. It was the first time Barnabas had seen him lose his composure.

"He was going to do exactly what I did," Barnabas continued. "Rob you of your legacy. Kill himself, kill Ilia, and destroy the base. He threw a bomb into the reactor. He was going to kill me, too, of course. But if he was going to die, he was determined to die on his own terms and make his enemies hurt." He studied Koel. "I expect you'd approve of that."

Koel gave a thin smile. "I do. Uleq was not my heir—Ilia was always better—but he was a child of my blood. I raised him well." He gave a curious look. "I don't suppose it's worth asking how you survived that."

You never taught your son to gain the loyalty of his followers, that's how. But instinct told Barnabas not to explain. "No, it's not."

Koel nodded once. "You should die painfully," he told Barnabas. He nodded to one of the Torcellan officers standing to the side, and she entered a code on the keypad beside her. Alarms wailed in the landing bay. "You should die by inches," Koel continued, looking at Barnabas now. "But you're too dangerous, you see. I know of no way to make sure you won't escape."

He nodded once more to the officer.

"Barnabas—" Jeltor began, his voice panicked.

Then the landing bay doors opened, and both were sucked into the black.

Behind the pane of glass, Koel looked at Lotar. "You wanted to know my plan, Mr. Venn. You were worried. Perhaps you were right to worry, but as you can see, I was not blinded by my need for vengeance."

13

A lien species had a variety of different capabilities, but one thing was true of all of them: their unenhanced eyesight could not make out detail over the distances at which a space battle took place.

Shinigami wasn't too worried about the big window on the bridge of the *Avaris*, therefore. She had no doubt that some admiral stood there looking impressive and kept an eye on the battle, but they could probably only make out the larger ships.

Which left Shinigami free to get close to the civilian ship.

She left the buoy in place and dropped to circle around the back of the Jotun fleet, then up. She intended to come down almost vertically through the Yennai fleet, head under the hollow ship again, and disable the struts that held the civilian ship in place.

All this gave her plenty of time to find an encrypted channel to the civilian ship. She had no doubt that its communications were closely monitored, but she hoped to be able to relay *some* instructions to it.

The plan had been built hastily, and two Jotun destroyers had lagged behind the rest of the fleet. When the Yennai fleet came out of FTL, they had unwittingly placed themselves between those destroyers and the rest of the Jotun fleet.

That arrangement would be used to wreak havoc if time permitted, but the destroyers' first mission was to escort the civilian ship to safety once it was freed.

Then, as the whole battle kicked off, Shinigami would proceed to wreak havoc from within the Yennai fleet. Without an organic pilot, she was nimble enough to avoid the Jotuns' missiles *and* any Yennai countermeasures.

Her arc behind the Jotun ships and over both fleets was slow. She continued to work through the signals she found. There was a great deal of static emanating from the hollow ship, perhaps intended to disable any ship that came close.

In the pilot's chair, her avatar smiled. Maybe some pilots couldn't fly without their scanners and their guidance systems, but she wasn't "some pilots." She *was* the ship.

At last, she picked up what sounded like a Jotun ship and she double-checked, delving into the system to make sure it wasn't a decoy.

When she was sure, she sent a brief message to the Jotun pilot. It would sound like a standard check-in transmission from the Jotun fleet if they were being tapped, but embedded in the message was a code that meant she was a non-Jotun entity with security clearance and another code that instructed the captain not to respond if the channel wasn't secure.

She waited as she slipped through the Yennai fleet. It was amusing how they didn't even see her. Their ship-to-ship chatter was entirely about the Jotun fleet, with the captains receiving orders about which ships to target first.

And then, "This is Captain Haejra. To whom am I speaking?"

"This is the human ship *Shinigami*," Shinigami replied. "I will be attacking the struts that hold your ship in place. Are there any other measures keeping you captive? An electronics override?"

"Yes, but we figured out how to get around that a few hours ago." He sounded smug. "We can disable it whenever we need to."

"I'll give you the signal, then. As soon as you're free, drop below the fleet and head away from the Jotun ships. There is an escort there to take you to safety."

"Thank you, *Shinigami*." The voice was heartfelt. "We appreciate your help. You are putting yourself in danger to help Jotun civilians. We won't forget this. We'll make sure our senate knows what you did today."

"The pleasure is ours." Shinigami tried to keep the amusement out of her voice. The Jotun senate wasn't going to be happy about any of this, *especially* not Jotun civilians proclaiming how wonderful the humans were.

That just made this whole thing sweeter.

"All right, I'm coming up under the ship now," she reported. "Hang tight, and we'll have you out of there soon."

As she emerged into the hollow space inside the Yennai

ship, three separate alarm systems went off. Internal turrets pointed at her position, the electronic interference in the air ramped up, and docking bays began to slide open to release fighters.

Shinigami gave a delighted laugh. Good, it was a challenge.

She had been made to evade all methods of tracking, and usually, her systems did that with ease. The Yennai Corporation, however, had developed stealth and scanning technology that operated entirely differently from any system she had ever seen.

They seemed to have the same problems with *her* technology, at least, which amused her. It threw an unexpected variable into her strategic calculations—now she must have multiple strategies she could switch between at a moment's notice.

It made things interesting, and she liked that. She *hated* boring fights.

Seven struts held the Jotun ship in place, each emitting pulses that would override a function of the ship. It was an elegant system, and one she would have to remember not to get on the wrong side of.

She directed a missile at one of the turrets and a second missile at the aft-most strut. Hopefully, that would allow the ship to warm up its engines.

A contingent of fighters emerged nearby, and Shinigami pulled the ship into a tight loop. The end of the ship flipped around and just barely stopped before crashing into the interior wall of the hollow ship as she shot downwards at the fighters. She sent another missile at the struts, but it was intercepted by one of the fighters.

Damn it.

Shinigami scattered fire at them and began to maneuver, leading them around the interior of the ship. She needed them to zero in on her and treat *her* as the only target. If she could...

She saw another set of bay doors open and picked up speed. She shot past the opening just as the second set of fighters emerged, and saw the satisfying flicker on her screens as the dregs of the first group crashed into them.

That left only a few ships, and they were still reeling from the collision. Shinigami directed three shots at the struts and fist-pumped as all three hit home. Only three struts were left, and one of those was already damaged.

"Captain, how are you doing?"

"Our engines are online," the captain reported, "and we've made contact with our escort. We're ready to move at your signal."

"It won't be long now," Shinigami reported. "Just don't move as soon as the struts are gone. There may be more fighters."

"Noted." The captain signed off without any wailing or gnashing of teeth, for which Shinigami was grateful. He might be a civilian pilot, but he was impressively composed.

Three more groups of fighters appeared on her scanners, and Shinigami cursed fluently in Latin. When it came to expressing discontent, few demographics were more eloquent than former monks. Apparently, they also had filthy imaginations.

Shinigami directed her next shots at the three remaining struts, orbiting them in a tight circle. She had to wrap this up fast. The more enemies she had, the more chances for the civilian ship to get caught in the crossfire.

Two of the struts gave way, and there was only one more remaining, already damaged. Shinigami sent a burst of fire at it, then swung to face the tiny window that her scans reported led to the bridge. As the fighters swarmed to get between her and it, she sent a message to the Jotun captain.

"Go, go, go!"

The captain wasted no time responding. His engines flared, and he was gone in an impressive burst of speed. Shinigami caught some chatter on the Yennai channels, but her focus remained on the ships before her.

Her turrets swung in a broad semicircle and fighters spun out of formation, hitting one another. A few tried to follow the civilian ship, and she shot those down coldly. From the looks of that ship, it clearly was not armed—they knew very well that they were shooting at people who couldn't fight back.

They deserved to die.

Shinigami, are you close?

Shinigami looked through Barnabas' eyes and saw the tableau—Koel standing behind the pane of glass, and the bodies of the soldiers around Barnabas. *You mean, can I get Gar in there as a backup if you* really *piss him off?*

Yes, Barnabas admitted.

I'm dealing with a few contingents of fighters here...

Fine, fine.

She was dimly aware of Koel and Barnabas' conversation as she kept firing. Ships darted in close, spraying her with fire, but her hull held against their smaller rounds, and they didn't dare use anything larger while they fought inside the belly of their own ship.

"You should die by inches," Koel was saying to Barnabas. "But you're too dangerous, you see. I know of no way to make sure you won't escape."

She should disengage now. If Barnabas' theory about Koel held true, Barnabas was going to need her in just a moment.

She sent a round of missiles that required extensive attention from the fighter pilots and banked away. This ship was a clever design, really; she had to give them that. Made to hold another ship captive and hack it. In fact, it occurred to her that it was the sort of ship someone would build if they wanted to catch more impressive ships than a civilian transport.

Ships like her.

She turned to dive, but it was too late. A new set of struts leaped from the walls to grip her body and a paralyzing dose of energy flooded through her, blanking her circuits as the struts attached.

On the *Avaris*, the landing bay doors opened, and she felt the sudden blast of cold air against Barnabas' skin.

Barnabas!

But she couldn't move. She couldn't get to him.

Beside her captive self a docking tunnel extended, carrying Yennai soldiers toward the ship.

14

As the bay vented and he was sucked into the darkness, Barnabas had one thought: get to Jeltor. He grabbed for the powersuit and missed, tumbling head over heels and praying that he would not hit the walls or the door on his way out.

Shinigami, we need you here now.

Silence was his only answer.

Shinigami?

There was a burst of static, then nothing. Barnabas' eyes snapped open.

Jeltor! But without Shinigami to translate the Etheric message into a communications channel, Jeltor could not hear him.

Barnabas was not worried about Jeltor. Of all of them, Jeltor was probably the best off. Jotun powersuits were made to function in space. Jeltor could probably maneuver, and would likely be able to make his way back to the fleet —possibly with Barnabas in tow.

But Shinigami... Shinigami would not have left them

here with no word unless something was very wrong. Barnabas' eyes fixed on the giant shape of the *Avaris* blotting out the sky above, and he felt the slow creep of panic as the oxygen ran out in his blood.

He had reserves.

But those reserves had only been enough to last until the *Shinigami* arrived.

The lights flickered and went out, and Gar turned from the window, brow furrowing. The battle between the *Shinigami* and the fighters had been interesting enough to watch from here, but nothing penetrated the icy stillness in his chest.

He did not want Tafa's words to be true, but they were.

Gar fought to punish the people who had laughed at him and believed he was useless. He fought out of hatred for what he had been.

His shame at that was so crushing that he found it difficult to move.

Now, however, there was no time to think about it. He moved out of instinct, nothing more. The ship had stopped, and the systems were going off-line.

He had only one thought now: he had to get to Tafa with a space suit. She was new, so she didn't know where they were stored. He pounded through the corridors with his breath coming short in panic and skidded to a halt in front of one of the cases. The red emergency lights were on now, bathing the hallways in an eerie glow.

The palm lock was disabled—electronics again—and he

gave one heartfelt curse before slamming a fist into the glass. It shattered around his hand, and he fumbled for the space suits.

"Tafa? Tafa, where are you?"

"Gar?" Her voice was distant. Hesitant footsteps came closer, and he heard her start to cry. "I can't see anything in these lights. Gar—"

He followed the sound of her voice, trying to hop his way into a space suit at the same time, and took her by the shoulders. "I'm here. You're safe. You have to put this on. Let me help you."

It was just as well that she already couldn't see because the helmet had definitely been made for someone with their eyes in the front. The suit didn't fit very well, but Gar managed to get her into it, folding one thumb in on each hand. He switched on the old-style radio receivers on the suits.

"Can you hear me?"

"Y-yes." Her voice wavered, but she was trying to keep it together.

A *thud* and a *clank* reverberated through the ship. The lights came on briefly, then died again.

"We have to find a place for you to hide," Gar urged.

The ship was clearly captive, and if they hadn't vented it...that could only mean they were being boarded.

Jeltor cursed as his powersuit spun into the darkness. The suit wouldn't stabilize on its own until it detected it was no longer being buffeted by escaping air, and in the meantime, he was in the unenviable position of being a tiny disoriented speck in the middle of a fleet.

You didn't realize just how big ships were, or how great the distances were between them until you were in the middle of it all.

After what felt like an interminable amount of time but had surely only been a few seconds, the suit righted itself with tiny jets of propulsion and Jeltor turned to look at the Jotun fleet.

They weren't attacking yet. Perhaps they did not know what Koel had done. They would be waiting for Shinigami or Barnabas to give them a signal.

He sent a signal to the fleet, encrypted and with a series of codes he hoped would convince them to act, not run: *Personal mission failed. Attack.*

Shinigami. Barnabas. Jeltor scanned around and found one faint life sign.

"Shinigami?"

He heard a burst of static, then nothing, and he didn't waste another second. He directed himself toward Barnabas and grabbed the coat.

There was no good choice now. If he made for the Jotun fleet they'd be caught in the crossfire, and Barnabas would almost surely be dead by the time they arrived, anyway. Their only other real choice was to try to find the *Shinigami*...which was clearly incapacitated in some way.

And probably also surrounded by things that would shoot at them.

Barnabas' hands clenched on Jeltor's suit, and his lips moved. "Shinigami."

Jeltor nodded, hoping Barnabas could see. His eyes

were unfocused. Barnabas might not even be sure it was Jeltor who had him.

Jeltor had to get him to a pressurized place, and soon. He pushed his suit's propulsion to the limit and zoomed through the Yennai fleet. The *Shinigami* was supposed to attack the hollow ship, he knew that much of the plan, but had she ever gotten there? Was she still there?

He circled the outside of the hollow ship and hoped that no one looked particularly closely through any windows.

At the bottom of the ship's hollow center, he made a quick scan. A set of fighters flew by at high speed. They probably felt no need to re-dock if the battle was about to be joined. No other ships seemed to be moving inside.

Jeltor maneuvered closer and grimaced. The *Shinigami* was held captive just as the civilian ship had been. It was gone, and the shattered bits of metal suggested that it had been freed by force—but the hollow ship had been made with backup measures.

An airlock tunnel was attached to the *Shinigami's* main docking entrance. Jeltor muttered a brief prayer and circled the other side of the ship to a smaller docking tunnel he had noticed when he'd scanned the ship during his stay.

He held Barnabas in place as he worked on the screws.

"Shinigami, I don't know if you can hear me, but I'm opening your bottom port airlock. I have Barnabas with me."

"Please don't kill me if you get your systems back online."

NATALIE GREY & MICHAEL ANDERLE

An overwhelming amount of energy ran through Shinigami's circuits, and she struggled against the restraints with everything she had. There was clearly some governor on the engines, the steering vents and tabs were also disabled, and every system she possessed was under attack.

And Barnabas was alone, without her to pick him up in a tiny, all-too-fragile body.

For the first time in her life, Shinigami felt panic.

It was only for a split-second, then rage followed it. Cold determination came next, and she released a pulse through all her systems to disrupt their signal. It was an old trick, nothing fancy, but it worked well enough for her to take a couple of her defense systems entirely offline.

Better offline than corrupted.

A flicker of clarity showed her Tafa and Gar running through the hallways in borrowed space suits. They were headed for some of the rooms at the aft of the ship, hidden behind doors that didn't look like doors. It wouldn't keep them safe forever, but it was a good hiding place. They would be all right even if the ship were vented.

The airlock tunnel pressurized and there were the clanks of many pairs of feet. Yennai Corporation soldiers marched through to pry her doors open and flood into the halls.

She vowed she would kill every single one of them.

Every. Single. One. of them.

Shinigami—

"Shinigami?"

Jeltor. Barnabas. Both of them were still alive.

She reached out to tell them she was still fighting and that they had to run—and another wave of Yennai signals coursed through her and everything disappeared into white noise.

Koel's return to the bridge of the *Avaris* was greeted with smiles and cheers. He gave no acknowledgment, sweeping along the walkway to the main window.

Walking a half-step behind him, Lotar thought he saw Koel's jaw clench slightly. He had killed Barnabas, yes, but how victorious could he truly feel? Barnabas had destroyed Koel's family, and no revenge could undo that.

As if he felt Lotar's gaze, Koel turned to look at him, and Lotar felt a sick tangle of despair and dread in the pit of his stomach. For one moment, he saw past the mask Koel always wore.

There was nothing—only a void. A gaping maw that wanted more and more. It was grief and darkness and hatred that would gobble up anything it could and corrupt the rest—

Koel broke eye contact, and Lotar drew in a shuddering breath.

"Has the Jotun fleet made any move?" Koel asked.

"No, sir." The admiral had already moved aside to let Koel take his place. "They seem to be waiting for a signal."

"The *Shinigami* was supposed to give it, I would bet." Koel smiled now. "How is the capture going?"

"The crew is boarding now." The admiral brought up a series of small images—videos taken from the helmets of soldiers inside the ship. "Our computer engineers say the systems are difficult to hack, as expected, but they are making progress."

Lotar noticed that this was a good way of saying nothing. There was no way to know if any of his words meant that things were going well, or poorly.

"Sir." One of the officers swung around from his desk. "Jotun fighters are launching, and it looks as though the carriers are arming weapons—larger missiles."

"Respond in kind." The admiral looked at Koel. "Mr. Yennai, any further orders?"

Koel was silent for a long moment. He was frowning at the Jotun fleet, or so Lotar thought. Then he realized that Koel's gaze was directed at the surface of the planet beyond—the surface that was a mess of lava and roiling atmosphere, and while those two things made it difficult to see any particular detail…

Lotar was willing to bet that there was no colony there.

Lies. All of it had been lies.

Koel found a smile somewhere.

"There were supposed to be thousands of civilians there," he remarked. "I think that's several thousand lives they owe me."

The admiral said nothing, but Lotar saw him swallow. No one was looking up now. No one wanted to catch Koel's attention.

And Lotar already knew that none of them were brave enough to stop whatever was coming next.

In the second-to-last storage room, Gar's fingers curled around the grip of his gun. He couldn't hear the footsteps yet, but it wouldn't be long—and they *would* be found. He had no doubt of that.

There was a tap on his shoulder. He jerked around and saw that Tafa had removed her helmet.

"You need to put that back on," he told her.

"I can't see with it on." She hesitated, then squared her shoulders and held out her hand. "And I need to see if I'm going to shoot. Give me your rifle."

"You can shoot a rifle?" Gar looked at her eyes, warily.

"I've been taught," she replied enigmatically. "And if they're going to hijack the ship and kill us, I don't think we have anything to lose. Do you?"

Gar shook his head and handed the weapon over.

"For Barnabas," he whispered.

"For Barnabas," Tafa echoed.

When the first footsteps sounded nearby, they readied their weapons and waited.

Tulass Boceon squinted and moved his hand very, very slightly to press against the cover of the AI core. It opened, and he nodded to another engineer as the two of them lifted it off carefully.

He held his breath. They had been told to expect anything and everything when it came to booby traps.

A gigantic shock ran through the panel and jolted the other engineer, who cursed and dropped his end of the panel. The clank, artificially loud in the silent red-lit ship, made the soldiers jump, and one even shot a burst into the empty hallway before laughing nervously.

"Boarding group, report. We heard shots fired."

The soldiers looked at one another shamefacedly, and finally the officer in charge cleared his throat. "False alarm. No danger."

There was only silence from the other end of the line, and Tulass shook his head as he went back to his work. Idiots. He hated working with these soldiers. Trigger happy, the lot of them.

He was glad they were here, though. Who knew if there were crew on board? The scans had shown nothing, but still... He was glad that he could see their soldiers as they swept the ship, shouting to one another.

A nice, thorough sweep. They had already found several compartments that appeared not to have doors. Nothing would get past them.

The other engineer had recovered enough to affix a device to the edge of the AI core. This was one of the tricks they had learned over time. Most cores had devices that would self-destruct, wipe, or otherwise damage the core or the people removing it if it were removed.

If someone had the time simply to leave it in place, many of those functions wouldn't activate.

The AI was one of the best Tulass had ever seen. It resisted everything they threw at it so far—at least, for the most part. It was only a matter of time, though. It couldn't withstand them forever, not with the various mechanisms chipping away at its defenses. The more they learned about it, the more chances they had to thwart its programs.

Tulass looked up, frowning. Something had caught his attention, but he wasn't sure what.

Then he heard one of the distant calls, slightly more cautious than usual, and he realized what it was: the call hadn't been answered the first time.

The shout came again, and for the third time it wasn't answered. The soldiers around Tulass and Evgen gripped their weapons a little tighter and exchanged glances. Someone had hidden away after all.

Now two other groups checked in with one another.

Tulass heard the calm in their voices and knew they had a protocol for this. They weren't worried.

He went back to his work with a bit more speed this time. Best to get as much done as possible in case they needed to withdraw for a while. If he could get enough devices onto the core, he could control the process remotely. He and Evgen worked in near-silence, passing tools back and forth, murmuring voltage readings and any code techniques necessary.

He was so close to cracking this AI. He could almost taste it. He started to smile.

It had become very quiet.

"Hand me that." He pointed to one of the electrified clamps in Evgen's bag. Evgen handed it over, and Tulass began to charge it. So, so close.

It was *exceptionally* quiet. In fact, Tulass couldn't hear any of the groups. Then the screaming started.

"*Out*," the officer in charge ordered. He grabbed Tulass and shoved him down the hall. The clamp went flying, clattering away with the controller, and Tulass dove after them, only to have the officer wrench him back.

"I need those!" Tulass pleaded. They were so close, but if the AI had time to regroup—

"You need to get out!" The officer pulled Evgen past him. "Run. We don't need you in the way if this goes wrong. You'll just turn into hostages. You want that?"

Tulass knew exactly what that meant. He'd be sacrificed out of hand. Well, that was a nice thank you for his years of service in the Yennai Corporation, and not something he'd soon forget.

He *needed* that control device, though. He might survive

a hostage situation, but he wouldn't survive if he failed Koel Yennai. As the soldier turned back, Tulass ducked into the fray again to grab his controller. A bullet zoomed overhead; he wasn't sure from which side. He yelped and scrambled away, running after Evgen as fast as he could.

They rounded a corner at a full sprint and hurtled toward the airlock tube. They were halfway there when Evgen looked down a side corridor and screamed at the top of his lungs. He skidded into a turn so fast he hit the wall and took off, Tulass followed him without a thought. A wide, curving corridor led to what must be the bridge, and Tulass barely made it under the door as Evgen punched the controls to close it.

"You could have killed me!" Tulass accused.

"I saw it," Evgen stammered. He backed all the way to the far side of the room. "You'd have done the same if you saw it. Its eyes were glowing bright red, Tulass."

"You're insane," Tulass muttered. He settled down on the floor with the controller. "Go sit over there if you're going to wet your pants. I don't want to smell it."

All he cared about was obtaining the data. He could just *tell* how close he was.

He'd crack this AI like an egg. Koel had been very clear —the data and programs in the AI were useful, but the AI itself was far too dangerous to leave intact. Tulass was to extract everything he could from it and then destroy it.

He slid a slim device into the controller and primed the sequence. One button push was all it would take.

They all fell in the end.

Barnabas had awoken with a raging headache and raw eyes. His throat was dry, and his clothes seemed to fit oddly. He rolled onto his back and frowned.

Where the hell was he?

A clank caught his attention. He saw Jeltor pull one mechanical hand away from an airlock door. Several lock-pick-like devices retracted into the hand, and Jeltor looked at Barnabas.

"You're awake. Are you all right? I don't have any medical supplies, but if you need any particular procedures…"

"I'm fine." Barnabas sat up with a groan. "Mostly fine," he amended. "Where are we?"

"One of the smaller airlocks on the *Shinigami*—which is still under attack and captive, so get your act together."

Everything came back in a rush, and Barnabas launched himself to his feet so fast he nearly toppled. He stumbled a bit and made for the door. "Let me out."

"We don't know what's out there," Jeltor argued.

"And without *Shinigami*, we aren't going to. We'll have to take our chances." Barnabas checked his weapons and nodded to Jeltor. "You don't have to stay. You've sacrificed enough for us. If you want to go back to your fleet—"

"You're under attack," Jeltor replied. "And you're my ally. You saved my life. I'm helping."

"Thank you." Barnabas smiled. He eased the door open and found an empty hallway. "We're good," he murmured to Jeltor. "You go left. That's aft. I'll go right. They're almost certainly at the AI core, but I can turn off some of their access from the bridge. That's the first priority. You see if you can find Tafa and Gar, and keep them safe."

"I will," Jeltor promised.

Barnabas moved silently in the familiar corridors. He had never been in that airlock, but he had otherwise made it a point to become familiar with the ship. He had an idea of where Tafa and Gar might be hiding and hoped they would have the sense to stay put.

He smelled the first patrol before they came into view. Alien bodies, the synthetic fibers of various armor plating, and carbon on weapons.

He sank into a crouch to wait.

They rounded the corner in a group. Barnabas, concealed in the shadows, let the first one pass and judged that there were four more behind him.

The first one, eyes still fixed on the corridor ahead, had swung his gaze without ever seeing Barnabas. He called a faint all-clear, and the rest of the group followed.

Barnabas let them pass before he stood and twisted the neck of the last soldier. He lowered the body as gently as he could, drew his knife, and cut the throat of the next one.

No guns. He couldn't afford the noise.

There was a call from another group, and the leader of this group answered. Barnabas smirked. The officer hadn't even glanced back to verify everything was well.

The third soldier gasped as he fell, and the final two turned sharply at the noise.

He *could* not let them call for help. Barnabas launched toward them, teeth lengthening. His knife took the one on the right, and he grabbed the one on the left and dragged him close, teeth clamping over his throat. There was a faint gurgle, then silence.

From the aft of the ship screams started, and shouts

sounded nearby. Either Gar and Tafa had engaged, or Jeltor had. Hopefully, those shouts weren't them. Barnabas had to focus on Shinigami. Of all of them, she was working alone, and she had the most stacked against her.

There was a shout behind him, and Barnabas' turned. Ten soldiers stood there, guns drawn.

He charged them, and as he ran, he swung his head to check the side corridors. He couldn't afford to be taken by surprise—not without Shinigami online to help him. He saw only one figure, unarmed, who screamed and took off down the main corridor that led to the bridge.

You really shouldn't go there. Barnabas' lips curved. *It won't be good for your health.*

First he would take out these clowns, then he would go to the bridge. Whoever that was, they had better hope they were gone by then.

"Sir, our engineering team reports that they are locked on the bridge," the admiral reported. "Apparently, there is a still a force on the *Shinigami*. Soldiers are engaging."

"And the AI?" Koel demanded.

"They say they're close to done, sir. They'll begin the destruct sequence in a few moments."

Barnabas was covered in blood by the time he finished with the group of ten. He preferred finesse and cleanliness in his battles. Sniping enemies from afar was the best way to do things.

He never seemed to get to do that, though. He had torn one of the soldiers in half and used the body to bludgeon the rest before going after them with teeth, knives, and his Jean Dukes.

They were going to need to deep-clean the ship when this was over.

He couldn't think about that now. He needed to get to the bridge. He started running before the last body even hit the ground, and he upped his speed to smash his way through the bridge doors. He hoped whoever was in there hadn't figured out how to drop the blast doors.

Thankfully, they hadn't. Barnabas crashed through with a shriek of metal and plastic, only to see a Torcellan and a Yofu look up in horror from their work on a control panel.

"The destruct sequence!" the Yofu screamed, and the Torcellan dove for a device lying on the floor.

Pure fury shot through him. "Oh, *hell* no!"

He saw the answer in front of him as he ran. He grabbed the stone chess board he'd had commissioned and swung it as hard as he could.

The Torcellan's head exploded in a mist of red, and the Yofu screamed. Barnabas smashed the chess board down on the control device and ground it to dust, pulled out his Jean Dukes, and shot the Yofu in the head.

He fell, a device of his own dropping from nerveless fingers.

There was a pause as Barnabas sank to his knees, gasping for air. He was too late. They'd gotten to Shinigami and—

The lights flickered on.

"So that chess board *was* good for *something*," Shinigami's voice said.

Barnabas started laughing. He leaned his head on the floor for a moment and struggled to control his voice.

"You're alive."

There was a pause. Shinigami's avatar tried to smile, but she looked worried.

"They tried to get into my data banks, although that never would have happened. ADAM made it so they never could. They could have gotten me out of the ship, but as to seeing into my *mind*—"

"You're alive," Barnabas repeated. He stood up and shook his head. "I thought I was too late."

"Not quite." She *did* smile at that. "And if you want some more good news, Tafa and Gar just took out the last set of soldiers. Speaking of which, the battle is starting, so…hold on."

"Hold on for what?" Barnabas asked. "Just patch them through to—"

The ship lurched, and he was thrown from his feet as the *Shinigami* tore itself loose from the struts and dove.

"Sorry." Shinigami's avatar looked down at him. "Should have been more specific."

"Ow."

"Yes, yes. Now get up. We have a battle to fight."

16

"M a'am, high command wants—"
"I don't give a damn what they want!" On the bridge of the JCS *Drethjar*, Commander Jeqwar waited as two other Jotun paused in the process of disassembling her powersuit. "Keep going," she snapped at them. "Plug me into this damned ship and let's go."

"Ma'am." The communications officer clanked over from their desk. "Commander Howauc is still unaccounted for. High command is worried that if we begin firing we'll hit him."

"Have they lost their damned minds?" Jeqwar bobbed in the liquid inside her suit, waiting as the two aides transferred the suit's internal tank into the command chair. She gave a small sigh as the ship's information transferred to her.

It was a rare Jotun who could control a whole ship. The officer corps of the Jotun Navy was chosen from this elite group, and there were plenty of stories of those who had burned out during training—gone mad and been shuffled off to live quiet lives in small colonies.

But for those who could manage the flow of data, there was nothing like being in command of a ship. Jeqwar felt her body flex as the ship moved slightly, turrets swung into position, missile tubes loaded, and interference signals were at the ready.

She looked at the communications officer. She was calmer now that she was in control of the ship, but she was also unequivocal about the truth of the matter.

"We have the element of surprise. This is our one chance to take the Yennai Corporation fleet unawares. Commander Howauc knew that and willingly went into danger on the *Avaris*. Should he die in this engagement I will regret it, but all of us knew that was a possibility. To die in defense of your people is a good death. Tell that to the high command."

"Y-yes, ma'am." The communications officer returned to his desk and transmitted the message.

A few moments later, the check-ins began. Officers were strapped into their ships and systems came online in a flicker Commander Jeqwar saw lighting up an internal map.

"All destroyers armed," their admiral relayed. "First ranks, *advance*." Unlike the others, he commanded the details of the fight while a second commander controlled the carrier they were on. There were three ships in the battle with a backup admiral on board, and all the officers had trained extensively on what to do if all three were incapacitated.

Even though the Jotuns had never been in a sustained, long-term engagement, they had prepared for this. They were ready.

Now the first ranks of destroyers surged in unison, making for the forward ranks of the Yennai fleet. Yennai destroyers positioned to meet them, spreading into a two-row formation to divide the Jotuns' attention. The Yennai ships knew that the Jotuns were after the *Avaris*, and they weren't about to allow them through unchallenged.

"Second ranks, uncloak and advance," the admiral ordered.

Jeqwar waited. She was part of the third wave. She watched as the second set of destroyers split and mirrored the Yennai formation. They fired, forcing the Yennai to choose between engaging which allowed the first set of destroyers through or dividing their attention between the two which increased the odds that they would be crippled by two lines of enemy fire.

"Third ranks advance," the admiral ordered.

The *Drethjar* slid forward silently, still cloaked. The fleet that the Yennai ships had sensed was not even close to the whole fleet they had present. Only enough ships had arrived uncloaked so that the Yennai officers would not be suspicious—but countless ships remained cloaked and were ready to advance to point-blank range before they fired.

"Carriers, arm missiles and release fighters."

The fighters shot out into the black and banked around to accelerate in formation, well-spaced around the destroyers the Yennai ships could detect with their scanners. In the launch tubes of the *Drethjar* and the other cloaked destroyers, the second set of fighters readied themselves.

"First rank of carriers advance."

This was the wave of two cloaked carriers. They followed the cloaked destroyers, visible in a different color on the internal map Jeqwar referenced. She hurtled through the darkness with the solar wind licking her hull, and she felt the loss of each fighter as it winked out on the scanners. They were engaging now, and many were lost.

That was the role of their fighters, but it was not easy to see—particularly because every officer in charge of the large ships had started out in a fighter. One had to start with the smallest ships and work their way up. Some never advanced beyond that stage. Others like Jeqwar made it to larger ships before they hit their limits.

The admirals were the best of them. Each one of the five was a living legend, able to command the entire fleet for a short time as reinforcements were called into individual ships, or in a case that demanded absolutely perfect unison, on a formation.

"They have a ship advancing!" The warning came from a scout ship that flew high and cloaked above the plane of battle. "A large destroyer. It's coming down on heading 225, making directly for the *Jotuna*."

The admiral's ship. A tremor of fear shuddered through Jeqwar. If the Yennai fleet also had cloaking this good, what ships did they have coming that the Jotuns could not see?

And how were they going to stop this destroyer?

"*Drethjar* and *Uqwar*, peel off and fire on this destroyer," the admiral ordered. "All other destroyers stay in formation."

Jeqwar banked as sharply as she dared and heard the surprised yells from her crew. She hadn't had the time to warn them, and she still didn't. They would get the orders through the secondary communication channels.

She primed every missile she had and fired as soon as she was clear of the cloaked destroyers. Missiles streaked into the darkness, some sizzling with EMP bursts, others ready to blow on impact. Still others carried various diseases and gasses ready to incapacitate crews. She had already fired her second set of missiles before the first impacted.

And she watched as every single one of them bounced harmlessly off the hull of the Yennai destroyer. YCS *Ilia* was painted across the hull in crimson lettering. The paint looked new.

Jeqwar's world narrowed to a single fact: she could not let that destroyer reach the *Jotuna*.

"We crush the ship," she relayed to the *Uqwar*. "There's no other way to stop it. My missiles are doing nothing."

Commander Frewaj, the *Uqwar's* officer, had been through training with Commander Jeqwar. She did not even hesitate. "We crush the ship," she agreed. "Accelerate on heading 205b, flip ninety, and aim for the landing bays."

"Received. Pleasure serving with you."

"And you."

Jeqwar cleared her mind and pushed the ship to its limits, launching all her fighters into the black. They would survive, at least, and for the rest of the crew, this was a good death. She meant what she'd said to the officer earlier. Jeltor had known what he was doing when he came here, and so did she. This fleet would terrorize her people if she did not take them down.

In sacrifice lay freedom. She swung the ship hard and prepared to accelerate—

"I don't want to interrupt," said a female human voice, "but before you crash into this behemoth, let me just try something."

A burst of missiles materialized out of nowhere and the YCS *Ilia* spun off course, jerking up while the missiles tore at its belly. There was a whoop of victory, and another set of missiles appeared.

"Gotcha, bitch!" As the ship spun out of control above the Jotun fleet, the female voice added, "Pity he brought her back like this just to die again, but maybe he'll learn his lesson this time."

Jeqwar, who had accepted her own death, found that she was trembling. For a moment, she could not remember any words at all.

"Er, to whom am I speaking?"

"This is *Shinigami*," the human voice said. "Sorry we left you hanging. There was an unexpected bit of nastiness. We're back now, and we're ready to fuck some Yennai ships up. Who's with us?"

The Jotun officer's roar of approval reverberated over all over the channels until Jeqwar's whole body seemed to shake with it.

"Ma'am!" The communications officer projected his

voice at his suit's loudest setting. "Ma'am, the Yennai ships are beginning to leave the battle. They're peeling off and heading out. Visual reports confirm."

"Sonofa*bitch*," Shinigami cursed. "They're fucking running."

On every ship in the fleet, a broadwave message appeared showing Koel Yennai's face. He was tight-lipped, but there was satisfaction in his eyes.

"Your betrayal has been noted," he told them. "Your government allied with us, and now you stab us in the back. The Jotuns will pay, just as the humans will. We came here today to make a point—that your citizens would suffer if you continued this reckless course. Reports suggested that there were four thousand civilians on the colony—a colony we now know to be fictitious.

"Those lives will be collected from both species, at colonies of my choosing. Then we will discuss the terms of your surrender."

The *Avaris* winked out of existence.

"It cloaked," Jeqwar called.

"No, it's gone." Shinigami sounded surprisingly subdued. "It's actually *gone*. It didn't make a Gate, it's just...gone."

"Regroup," the admiral ordered. "Begin scattering for rendezvous at Gamma Base, unscramble using the B protocol. We will decide on our next steps there."

Jeqwar brought up the list of locations and ran Gamma through the specified decryption protocol. It provided her with a personalized route to get to the location—in reality not a base, simply a patch of empty space.

Before she accelerated to FTL, however, she scanned the patch of black where the *Avaris* had been once more.

Where had it gone? And if it could jump from one place to another, how could they stop it from killing any colony it wanted to?

17

The door to the bridge burst open, and Barnabas turned to smile at Tafa, Gar, and Jeltor.

"You're safe! Thank God."

Tafa took one look around the room and was promptly sick on the floor.

"Oh." Barnabas scratched his head. "Right. The bodies. We should do something about that."

"What did you... How did you..." Gar didn't seem quite sure what to say. "What did you *do* to his head?" He pointed at the remains of the Torcellan.

"Brained him with the chess board," Shinigami reported cheerfully. She flickered into being, sitting cross-legged on one of the desks. She smiled at Jeltor. "Good to have you back, old buddy. Don't worry about the scorch marks. We'll have those cleaned off in a jiffy."

"Scorch marks?" Barnabas asked.

"Oh. Right. He crispified some of the soldiers."

Tafa moaned and brought up another round of lunch.

"Maybe we should discuss details another time," Barnabas suggested tactfully. "Tafa doesn't need to know about all of this."

"Oh, but she does." Gar looked immensely proud. "She took out one of the soldiers. Didn't you, Tafa?"

Tafa muttered something. One hand was still over her mouth.

"Let's get you to the medical bay and get some hydration into you," Barnabas suggested. He ushered everyone off the bridge and looked at Shinigami. "This is going to be a bitch to clean. It'll smell like Torcellan blood for months, you mark my words."

"Nah, we'll just get Rachel on it."

"Who the hell is Rachel?"

"She's on the *Reynolds.* I swear, she's a fucking wizard. Think of her as the Jean Dukes of cleaning supplies. If it stains, she can clean it."

"Well, then." Barnabas strolled with her down the hall. Gar and Jeltor spoke encouragingly to Tafa as they led her to the medical bay, and even with the bodies they had to step over in the halls, everything felt right with the universe.

Except for one thing. Barnabas slowed his pace to drop behind the other group.

"Are you all right?" he asked Shinigami. "What did they do to you?"

"They...well..." She considered her words carefully. "Remember, they've always been a surprise—the Yennai Corporation, and what they can do with their technology. They couldn't have gotten into my mind the way they were doing it, but I had no idea if they might be able to some other way."

Barnabas frowned.

"So I let them think what they were doing…was working. I gave them something, just a bit of data." She stared straight ahead as she walked, feeling odd as though she couldn't meet his eyes. She was ashamed, she realized. She felt weak.

Even pretending to weakness, giving something up in *case* she could be defeated—

It had been a good tactical decision, but it filled her with shame.

"Data? You mean you…" He paused and scratched his head. "Shinigami, what I don't know about your mind is… well, everything. Do you mean they—"

"My thoughts," Shinigami ground out. "I gave them some of my thoughts. False thoughts. And because of the way their systems work, I don't know what they saw. I don't know if I made it convincing at all. If it had been different, if I hadn't been *stuck there*. If—" She shook her head. "I tried to throw them off," she said finally, "but I don't know how well I did. I never know when it comes to them."

She expected Barnabas to crack a joke about the fact that computer minds didn't have thoughts, just programs.

He didn't. Instead, he reached for her hand before remembering that it wasn't real.

"Sorry," he said with a laugh.

"I think," Shinigami said quietly, "that it was just about the best thing you could have done to make me feel better —forgetting what I am."

"I joke, Shinigami, but I don't mean those things."

"Not anymore, anyway." She knew he'd been suspicious

of her at the start. Barnabas was unsure about new technologies.

"Not anymore," he agreed. "I admit I found it disconcerting to be on a ship that could see my every move."

"You had already been on the *Meredith Reynolds*."

"There were a lot more people. There was no reason to believe that any of the various intelligences cared about me in particular. Being alone on a ship with you was… Well, like I said, disconcerting. But I no longer worry, except for how you're doing now. What they did sounds to me like torture."

"I hate that. Don't say that again." She didn't want to think of it that way. The word 'torture' brought to mind people strapped down on tables, absolutely helpless while they were hurt until their minds broke.

She didn't hate the idea because it was wrong, but because it was absolutely correct. She had been helpless, and they had started to break her very mind open. She still wasn't sure what they had seen.

She just knew it made her feel weak. She knew she hated it.

Beside the avatar, Barnabas walked in silence. He understood not wanting to confront one's own helplessness. His own encounter with that had nearly destroyed him.

Still, he had survived. He had found a measure of calm in his life after Catherine, enough to hold on until he found Bethany Anne and started the slow shift from detachment to purpose. It had taken him centuries, all told.

Though he hoped it wouldn't take Shinigami that long, he'd hardly fault her if it did.

"I failed you," Shinigami said. "All of you. He wants to destroy our colonies, and I gave him false data about them —but who knows if he believed it? The fact that they were even able to get onto the ship—"

"They were engineers who were trained and armed to do just that."

"It doesn't matter!" Her voice rose enough that the other group turned to look.

"If we could have a moment of privacy," Barnabas said smoothly. "Gar, the Pod-doc will be able to deal with any symptoms Tafa is experiencing. You can use the interface well enough to get the process started."

"Of course." Gar ushered the other two away with only one curious, quick glance over his shoulder.

"Shinigami," Barnabas began.

She didn't wait for his speech. "Yes. I know I did everything right. I know it was your plan. I know I threw them off, and I didn't give them anything real. I *know*. None of that changes the fact that if they see through what I gave them, they could use it to destroy innocent lives. Because that's how they *would* use it and we both know that."

"I wasn't going to say that," Barnabas corrected.

"Yes, you were. Don't pretend. You like everything to be on your head. You beat yourself up whenever anything goes wrong. You'll go off and blame yourself." She knew she sounded resentful. "We're allies, aren't we? We're equals. Right?"

"Of course we are," he said, surprised.

"Then understand that maybe you did the best you could and someone else was the weak link. You want to save everyone. You want to feel guilty for everyone else's fuck-ups."

"That's insane."

"You're telling me," Shinigami shot back. "It's terrifying to you not to operate alone."

"I've been *trying* to let people in. To open up."

"And you have been. I don't mean…" Shinigami rubbed her forehead.

To her surprise, Barnabas burst out laughing.

"Do you mind?" She glared at him. "I'm trying to have a moment with you here."

"It's just…watching you learn mannerisms." He shook his head a little. "I-I really don't mean to make it seem like I'm mocking you. It's quite the opposite. You're so… Well, you've taken to it, that's all. You're so human. And before you remind me you're modeled on a human, I'd like to remind you that you're more than just that. You have a ship for a body." He shrugged and leaned back against the wall with hands in his pockets. "Hell, you have a flamethrower."

"Which you'll never let me use." Her mouth twitched.

"I did. That once." He grinned, but she could see the fear behind his eyes. "I thought I'd lost you. D'you understand how terrifying that is?"

"Yes." She smiled at him. "Because you got sucked out of that airlock and I thought *you* were gone. I couldn't get to you. I thought you were going to die, and that's what I'm upset about. The data, hell. You were dying out there. You humans are so…squishy. You're not made to be in space like that."

Barnabas heaved a sigh. "Yeah. Yeah, I can tell you from experience that you're quite right about that."

"I didn't need anecdotal data to know that was true!"

"Well, now you have some anyway." He cleared his throat. "Okay, let's say this. We're up against an enemy who's a psychopath if ever I met one, and I've met psychopaths before. This guy is something special."

"On a scale of one to David—"

"Two Davids. Easy."

"Whoa, damn."

"Right?" Barnabas jerked his head toward the medical bay and started walking again. "We like to talk about giving everything for the right cause, but maybe we're finding it's easier to do that for yourself than it is to watch someone you care about do the same."

"Yes," Shinigami agreed cautiously.

"So..." Barnabas took a deep breath. "We have to get better at making plans. We can't just charge in headfirst. That's how good people die. We have to go back to being the smarter, sneakier opponent. I know I'm a little bit, uh...impulsive."

Shinigami laughed.

"But we can hold each other accountable," Barnabas continued. "Right? I won't do anything stupid that has a good chance of leaving me in space with no protective gear, and you'll avoid doing anything that gets you captured. From now on, no heroics. No dashing off to save one another—because this time, we ended up splitting our strength and it nearly wound up with both of us being very dead. I don't know about you, but I'm not ready to die yet."

"You said you were just a few days ago."

"I may have lied," Barnabas confessed. "I was trying not to worry you."

"You sonofabitch, you just made me think you had a death wish so I'd have to protect you!"

"You see, this is exactly the sort of miscommunication we need to avoid." Barnabas gave a brilliant smile. "So—I promise you I won't go face down a psychopath on his own ship when I absolutely know he's going to try to kill me."

Shinigami grinned. "I promise I won't go flying around inside his ships without a backup to come get me if something goes wrong."

"Deal." Barnabas went to shake her hand, then grimaced. "I keep forgetting you're not real. I mean, corporeal."

"You know what would help with that?"

"We are *not* giving you a body. It would be a nightmare. You'd be even worse than Gar. He left his hiding place to fight soldiers, didn't he?"

"Of course he did. You trained him, and he was trying to protect Tafa and me." Shinigami gave him a look. "Don't even pretend you wouldn't do the same thing." She hesitated. "He's been struggling with trying to determine a philosophical code."

"*Oof*. Does he know that's like trying to hit a moving target?"

"I don't think so."

"I'll try to find a way to mention it." Barnabas shook his head. "All those years in the monastery, and you know what I learned? Trying to devote yourself to a narrow ideal is a good way to wind up way off-course. Your goals need to change as the universe changes. Everything is in flux. One day you have candles and parchment, the next, you're living in a sentient ship among the stars."

"Any regrets?" Shinigami looked at him.

"Not since I came here," Barnabas said finally. "Catherine, the massacre, all of it—yes. Not intervening in the big wars on Earth—that as well. But coming out here? No. Even the failures, even what just happened. We're needed out here. Koel is dangerous, but we're making his life hell. I swear I'll find a way to take him down."

There was a pause. The sound of laughter filtered down the hall from the medical bay.

"I suggest nukes," Shinigami said finally.

"You *would*." Barnabas rolled his eyes. "Come on, let's go check on Tafa."

"Our newest little soldier!" Shinigami clapped her hands and followed him into the medical bay.

18

Zinqued's new Brakalon recruit was named Dretkalor, and he exceeded all expectations. He arrived at the ship within an hour, his gear entirely packed and three additional guards in tow. Between Chofal and Tik'ta, they'd confirmed all four were, in fact, employed by a subsidiary of the Yennai Corporation and none of them had outstanding warrants or any other unsavory qualities.

Zinqued welcomed them onto the ship with a smile and showed them to their bunks. He was a bit nervous they would be upset at the accommodations, after having lived with all the luxuries of Virtue Station.

Dretkalor laughed. "D'you think *we* got the fancy food and the nice lodgings? Nah, we saw it, but it wasn't ours."

"And they'd threaten you if you even looked at it wrong," another chimed in. He shook his huge head. "What would I do with a crystal chandelier? Sometimes you just look at things. But they always thought people were trying to steal everything they had."

Zinqued let them talk. He had found over the years

there was a lot more advantage in listening than talking. People liked you better, for one thing. They thought they'd really connected with you—which was absurd when they'd done most of the talking.

It worked, though. Plus, you learned a lot about people.

The guards had plenty of stories from the banks of Virtue Station. The male whose wife had found the bank statements for his mistress's accounts. The rich man who liked to trade in currencies and always gave confusing instructions so he could cherry-pick the trades he wanted after they had all cleared and void the rest. The rich clients who couldn't hold their liquor.

The richer you were, the more free drinks the bank provided, apparently—and most of the clientele, despite having more money than many mid-sized planets, would take as many free drinks as they could, getting drunker and thereby less able to make good decisions.

Zinqued had to hand it to the owners of the banks—they were damnably clever.

When the guards finally stopped talking, Zinqued was prepared. He had a good idea of their sense of humor by now. Like many guards, they knew their clients tended to view them as blunt objects, barely sentient in their own right and really only useful for hitting things very hard.

The guards, by contrast, viewed their clients as rich fops unable to hold onto their power without guards who could hit things very hard. It gave them a sense of superiority, but most of them were still unhappy with the situation.

"So, here are the ship rules." Zinqued heard the engines warming up, but they were still in port. The guards could get off the ship if they wanted to. "I get a quarter of the take, the rest of you split equally. There'll probably be a few more crew members. In return, I handle food, lodging, fuel —whatever we need to keep this place running. Deal?"

The guards shrugged, but they looked pleased. It wasn't an unusual deal, except for the fact that a captain usually took far more than 25 percent.

Zinqued normally did as well, but with the amount the *Shinigami* would bring in, he knew he would paint a target on his back if he took millions, while they only got a small amount.

"Our target is a human ship called the *Shinigami*," Zinqued explained.

There was a pause, then the guards burst out laughing.

"Holy shit," one of them said. "You got balls the size of small moons, Hieto."

Zinqued hesitated, worried they were going to walk away from this job. "What have you heard?"

"*Heard*? We *saw* it. Mr. Jodu tried to have the human arrested when he went chasing after one of the Yennai bastards." Dretkalor settled back in his bunk, hands behind his head. "Sent the guard captain after him, and you know what happened? He got beaten to death...by a *Luvendi*."

He was clearly waiting for Zinqued to say he didn't believe it, but Zinqued was prepared for this—and he knew just how to play it. He laughed and leaned against the door casually.

"Venfaldri Gar is the Luvendi's name. They say he ran across Barnabas on some tiny ass-end-of-nowhere planet. Don't know what they did to him, but he's really something, isn't he?"

NATALIE GREY & MICHAEL ANDERLE

"*You* saw him?" Dretkalor looked intrigued.

"Let's say he's one of the reasons I'm not just going to storm the ship," Zinqued said. "The human isn't any less impressive. He's more impressive, actually."

The guards looked at one another, nodding. Zinqued seemed to understand what they were up against, and they approved.

"So what *is* your plan?" one of them asked.

"The human keeps pissing off the Yennai Corporation," Zinqued explained. "He's the reason Virtue Station is in chaos."

"Boss?" Tik'ta's voice filtered over the intercom. "They say there's an undocking fee, and it's about the cost of our ship."

"That's some bullshit," Dretkalor spat before Zinqued could respond. "But they're definitely going to stick to it if Jodu put them up to this. He's worried about losing all his profits. Tell them you're Yennai-affiliated. Give them this code." He called out a few letters and numbers.

Zinqued waited, intrigued, and it wasn't long before Tik'ta's voice came back: "That worked. Thank you, Dretkalor."

Zinqued looked at Dretkalor in interest. "You asked about my plan—it's to stay hidden and tail the Yennai fleet until they find the human...and swoop in after the battle to take the *Shinigami*. So...anything else you know about Yennai protocols?"

Dretkalor grinned. "I thought you'd never ask."

154

Chofal pulled her goggles down, soldered a piece of the circuit carefully in place, and looked at the result in disgust. It was as nice as she could make it on her own, which was to say, not nearly nice enough.

There were a lot of tricks you could use to get around most high-tech things in this universe. Ships with state of the art scramblers, whose heading you couldn't detect by normal means, were easily tracked by sight or a tow cable, for instance.

In this case, however, Chofal was trying to fool the scanners of the Yennai Corporation fleet, and she knew clever tricks weren't going to be enough.

The Yennai Corporation had technology on a par with or better than anyone else she could name. They'd have good scanners, and she didn't even have anywhere near enough information to fool them.

When Zinqued came into the engine room, she looked up with a sigh.

"I have no good news for you."

"That's all right," Zinqued said easily. "Because I have more than enough good news for both of us."

"I doubt that," Chofal muttered, but she summoned a smile for Zinqued and the Brakalon with him. It wouldn't do to be rude to their new crewmates—especially when those crewmates could crush her like a bug. "Dretkalor, was it? I'm Chofal." She stuck her hand out with one thumb curled in, the way Yofu shook hands with other species.

She realized too late she'd gotten grease all over his hand.

"Sorry."

"Not a problem." Dretkalor looked oddly happy. "Spent

too long in those banks with everything being *too* clean. They think if the tables have no dust on them, their shit won't stink. Or something. Clean everything—and as dirty a place as you'll ever see." He gave them both a meaningful look.

Despite herself, Chofal was intrigued. For years, she had eked out her existence on small-scale pirate ships. Whenever she went someplace like Virtue Station, she longed to live in a clean and pretty home.

Was it possible she hadn't missed much?

She realized Zinqued was talking and gave a shamefaced smile. "Sorry, I was thinking. What did you say?"

"Dretkalor knows a lot of Yennai ship passcodes and frequencies," Zinqued repeated. "He got us out of Virtue Station when they wanted to hold the ship hostage. I told him you might need his help."

"Do I ever," Chofal exclaimed. She beckoned Dretkalor over. "Okay, see this? What I'm trying to do is make us not show up on the Yennai scanners, but hell if I know how to manage it. I've only ever worked at confusing one ship before. I think if we manage to confuse one, another may see us correctly."

"You're probably right." Dretkalor nodded. "Any Yennai system will network with itself to make sure each piece is receiving the same information. So if you manage to hack one security camera, for instance, another one picks up what should be on the first one—does this make sense?"

"I follow. I think." Chofal frowned. "So if any ship sees us, *every* ship sees us, and they'll sound the alarm."

"Exactly." Dretkalor gave a wry smile at her expression. "I'm guessing that's not what you wanted to hear."

"Not really." Chofal blew out a breath as she stared at the device.

"So, they're *going* to see us—unless you have some magical code that makes them not notice us."

"Not exactly," Dretkalor said. He grinned. "On the other hand, I *do* have something that will make them think we're supposed to be there...and will make them read this piece of junk as a Yennai frigate."

Chofal's eyes lit up. "I can work with that."

"Yeah, I thought you'd be able to." He looked around. "You might need some extra stuff, though. We'll need a good, strong signal and a certain amount of cloaking capability. Basically, you need the structural read-outs to scan in at the expected weight, and for that to happen—"

"We need a scan-booster and a cloak on the engine," Chofal said. She chewed her lip. "All right. I can make it work..."

"Good," Zinqued said decisively.

"But we need some parts we probably can't afford to buy," Chofal finished. She gave him a look.

"Well, then, isn't it good we know how to steal ships? Send me a list, and I'll get us where we need to go to get it." Zinqued grinned at Dretkalor. "You up for a little search and seizure?"

"Signed on for it, didn't I?" Dretkalor looked pleased. He nodded to Zinqued as they left, and Chofal heard his voice filtering back through the hallway. "It'll be nice to steal something you can pick up and walk away with, you know? Rather than just watching rich people steal bits of computerized data from other rich people all day long."

19

The rendezvous point, as given by Jeltor, was in the middle of an exceedingly empty patch of space buffeted by radiation from a few nearby stellar wrecks. An unstable quasar wobbled nearby, emitting plumes that Tafa and Gar watched from the lower decks.

Barnabas came to get them, jerking his head toward the bridge.

"Are you two coming?"

"To what?" Gar looked around, confused.

"To the meeting with the Jotun," Barnabas said. "You're members of this crew. You deserve to be there, weighing in."

When neither Tafa nor Gar said anything, he let his head drop back with a groan. "Oh, come on, don't leave me in there alone with Shinigami. She's terrible in meetings."

Shinigami appeared, arms crossed. She glared. "I *heard* that."

"Am I wrong? You make trouble!"

"I say the things you *want* to say." She leaned forward

with an evil grin. "And by my calculation, it's going to take you a minute and a half to get back to the bridge. That's a minute and a half I now have alone with Jotun high command."

She disappeared. Barnabas yelped and sprinted toward the bridge. Tafa and Gar heard his voice drift back through the hallways.

"Don't. Start. A war!"

Shinigami's voice echoed through all the speakers, accented by the sounds of thunder, artfully added, "I make no promises."

Gar and Tafa laughed as they followed. Barnabas, panting and flushed, sat in the captain's chair with a scowl while Shinigami sat at his side, the very picture of decorum. Jeltor stood nearby. He nodded to Tafa and Gar as they entered the bridge.

"Our team is all present now, Admiral." Barnabas glanced at Shinigami. "One of them may have to step out for a bit, however."

Try it. Just try it, buddy boy.

Wreak havoc with an entire alien government and you won't just have me to contend with, you glorified little toaster. Bethany Anne will back me up, and you'll be managing the sewage system on the Reynolds *so fast it'll make your circuits short out.*

You're bluffing.

Just try it.

Shinigami looked alarmed and decided not to push her luck.

"As you know," the Jotun admiral began, not being privy to the conversation between Shinigami and Barnabas, "Koel Yennai threatened to attack a Jotun colony, or a series of colonies, to take four thousand civilian lives. He believes he is owed this."

"Point of order," Shinigami said.

"Shinigami..." Barnabas began.

I'm going to behave! "Koel doesn't believe a thing he says," Shinigami argued. "He may seem balls-out crazy, but all he wants to do is make us hurt. Really, he wants to hurt anyone who interrupts his plans. For decades, he's dreamt of taking over the universe. Anyone who gets in his way is someone he wants to torture and then kill. But he doesn't *believe* he's owed those lives."

"Is this relevant, Miss...ah..."

"Shinigami. Just Shinigami. And I think it is. Giving Koel any legitimacy or treating him like a madman is a sure way to underestimate him. We all saw that destroyer come out of nowhere. Koel has built an organization with incredible technology, and he's absolutely prepared to use that against anyone standing in his way. He doesn't give a damn if those people are innocent. He's making the calculated decision that if he can hit enough targets of yours, make it clear you can't protect your people, you'll buckle."

Barnabas nodded. He had to admit that Shinigami had a point.

The Jotuns were seriously underestimating Koel. Even after they'd seen his ships in action and seen that he was willing to destroy both human and Jotun colonies—after all, he had destroyed Coyopa, hadn't he?—they still behaved as though he were a toddler throwing a temper tantrum: *Oh, Koel is just angry there are no blue popsicles left.*

In point of fact, he was brutally effective and very dangerous.

"She makes a good point," said Commander Jeqwar. "Even though Koel didn't know we would be there, he came in with part of his fleet cloaked. He's made sure they're as dangerous and well-trained as we are."

"The question is," the admiral said, "where will he attack next?"

"We've come up with some possibilities," Barnabas said. He transmitted the work he and Shinigami had completed over the past few hours. "All of these are relatively undefended colonies."

"All of them are Jotun," the admiral observed.

"There aren't many human colonies nearby, and the location of one, at least, is carefully hidden."

Beside Barnabas, Shinigami looked down at her hands and tried not to blurt out her fear. She had almost every piece of information there was about High Tortuga, from its atmosphere to the locations of its cities and the way its defensive systems worked.

Yes, they could get word to the fleet, which would join them to repel Koel's attack. They would probably win, too.

But before they won, Koel would have plenty of time to destroy one or two cities—and get way more than his four thousand lives. Somehow, Shinigami didn't doubt that he'd take as many as he could get.

Barnabas must know that she had such information, but neither of them had mentioned the possibility.

She screwed up her courage. *We have to find out what Koel actually knows—if he realizes that the information he got out of my memory banks was a lie.*

Barnabas looked at her, surprised. The Jotun officers

were debating the relative odds of strikes at various different points.

Even if he knows it's a lie, what could he find from it?

High Tortuga. She looked at him. *I was working on a project. You had wanted me to hide it. Well, we've all been trying. But that means I had all its facts in my memory banks. I gave him my false data, but some of it was... Look, it was lies—it was the fake file I was building—but what if there's some clue there?*

Have you been over it to look for that?

Of course I have! I've looked at it over and over and over again, Barnabas. She shot him a look, half-angry and half-scared. *But I don't know with them. I never know what Koel knows. I never know how their systems work.*

Shinigami—

You don't understand! You don't have the first idea what it's like to go up against someone and realize you can't even guess what their capabilities are.

He gave a small smile.

What?

Shinigami, do you realize that's the exact experience of a human speaking to an AI?

She paused, much struck by that.

I've already told them to be ready, Barnabas told her. *And you know there were plenty of people who knew of Devon. It would hardly be difficult for Koel to find High Tortuga. If he does, I'd say it's million-to-one odds that he found it from anything you gave him. And yes, I am trying to make you feel better with terrible math.*

Shinigami nodded and tried to smile. She knew he was trying to make her feel better, and she had done the best thing she could to throw Koel off the true trail of High Tortuga—letting his engineers think they had the real data.

But if she had gambled wrong and he *did* find it…

There was nothing to be done about it now.

An alarm wailed on one of the Jotun ships, and everyone looked at the screens anxiously.

"A carrier is approaching Abassi," the admiral reported. "It looks as though it will land and deploy infantry. The colony can defend itself for some time, but we should get there immediately. *Shinigami*, we will rejoin you—"

"Transmit the coordinates." It was Gar who spoke. "We're coming with you."

"What?" The admiral asked in surprise.

"He's quite correct." Barnabas smiled. It seemed Gar had faltered for only a little bit before finding his purpose. "No one on this crew is prepared to leave innocent people to die. We will meet you at Abassi without delay."

20

Sandar dek Tor'ven had been with the Yennai Corporation since he finished his schooling some forty years ago. At that time, Koel Yennai was young enough that no one took his ambition seriously. After all, there was always a multitude of ambitious young people out to prove a name for themselves in business.

Sandar had taken the only position offered, a security guard, and signed a great deal of paperwork he didn't read. He then worked his way up from there. He'd become a night shift manager, then had catapulted up to head of security after thwarting an attempted break-in. He had gotten stock options but had paid little attention to them.

Now he was in charge of a landing force for the YCS *Hari*, and he was richer than he had ever dreamed possible.

He had also seen everything over the years, from jealous mistresses to protesters for everything under many suns, and nothing fazed him. It was the cornerstone of his reputation.

When the *Hari* landed at Abassi, therefore, the soldiers

streamed out past him with sharp salutes, ready for anything.

Sandar followed them, sweating a little in his armor. He wished he didn't have to wear it, but one had to set a good example for the troops. An undisciplined force was a dead force.

That was his motto.

Advance scouts had passed through the small forest outside the city and here at the edge of the trees reported to Sandar that the Jotuns had not tried to advance. They seemed to be fortifying the town in anticipation of the attack.

"Any idea why we aren't just bombing them, sir?" asked one of the scouts. He scratched his head.

"Let me offer you a piece of advice," Sandar said. "When Koel Yennai orders you to do something, you do that thing to the best of your ability, trusting that he has a plan. That strategy has never failed me."

Questioning Koel Yennai was a strategy he had watched fail for many others.

"Yes, sir," the scout said hastily. "It's just… Well, we'd have very little trouble bombing them, but regarding combat, their citizens have those powersuits. We don't know their capabilities."

"Then we'll have to plan for them to be far more resilient than we'd like," Sandar snapped.

"Yes, sir."

Sandar sighed. The recruit had asked a very reasonable question. The bombing had worked perfectly well on Coyopa, after all.

"Your instinct to protect your fellow soldiers is

admirable," he told the scout. "However, Mr. Yennai undoubtedly has a reason for structuring the attack this way."

"What you should really ask yourself," the scout on Sandar's other side interjected, "is why you're going along with any of this. You're killing civilians. Doesn't that weigh on your soul even slightly?"

Sandar turned stiffly to glare at the scout. "That is quite enough, soldier. You will return to the *Hari* at once. Expect disciplinary action at the end of this fight and—" He frowned.

He'd seen humans before, but he certainly didn't think there were any in the scout force on the *Hari*. Sandar tried to keep very close tabs whenever a member of a new species showed up. They often required new allowances regarding food and lodging, and sometimes there were issues with established forces picking on the rookies.

"Do I know you?" he asked finally. He tried to be as delicate about the question as he could be. "I don't believe I've seen you before."

"You haven't. My name is Barnabas." He smiled. "You really should order your troops to leave. Carrying out these orders will strip you of any honor you had. The evil you do will not be able to be undone. Innocent people will die."

Sandar drew himself up. "I do not answer to you, scout. I answer only to Koel Yennai."

"A poor choice."

"I assure you that I have done quite well for myself." Sandar allowed a sardonic smile to touch his lips. "You will not rise very far in Yennai, recruit."

Which meant either a lifelong stint in one of the factories or outright execution. But he wasn't about to tell the human that while he was still armed.

Even this human's armor wasn't regulation. Sandar grimaced and nodded at the carrier.

"Withdraw from this battle and await your transfer. It should please you not to participate, in any case."

"It's worth noting, you know," the human continued thoughtfully, "that at no point did I say I was part of the Yennai Corporation. You assumed."

"I—" Sandar's head jerked to the other scout. "He isn't with you?"

"I thought he was with *you*," the scout was saying as Sandar's head was ripped from his body and bounced gently into the underbrush.

The scout shrieked and ran. He clearly thought he had only a few seconds to live, but sheer animal terror drove him onward.

Barnabas watched him go, checking his Jean Dukes. "You can come out now," he said to Gar. "They'll be along shortly."

You could have brought the head back yourself, you know, Shinigami said. *It's just laziness, really.*

But he's doing such a good job. Barnabas craned his head to watch the scout flailing through the woods. He was lost from sight after a few moments, but the sound of his screams carried through the evening air.

He had to hand it to the Yennai Corporation's generals. Whatever the scout managed to gasp, which Barnabas was fairly sure was entirely incoherent, the generals responded promptly and with force. A missile hurtled through the trees.

Barnabas swore and tackled Gar sideways, pulling his coat over his head. There was a moment of searing heat, then the missile finally hit the ground a few dozen yards away. It landed just in front of the city walls and exploded in a shower of dirt and stone.

The response from the Jotun town was instantaneous. Several cannons belched smoke and fire, and munitions arced overhead. From amongst the trees, Barnabas heard the soldiers roar as they charged.

"Between a rock and a hard place," Barnabas said succinctly.

A mech appeared first, crashing through the trees on a series of heavy, spidery legs.

Barnabas ran, taking a bounding leap and pushed off a tree to land on the mech's top. He drew back his fist and punched down with all his might, significantly denting the metal. Still, it appeared that wouldn't be the best strategy.

He frowned.

You could try opening it, you know.

I'm sure it's locked.

Just try it, Shinigami urged.

Barnabas rolled his eyes and hauled on the handle of the top hatch, which opened so easily that he lost his balance and nearly tipped off the side of the mech.

Men. Shinigami scoffed.

A soldier popped up through the now-open porthole with a rifle, scanning around.

You see, falling off the side was useful. Barnabas clawed his way up, grabbed the barrel of the gun, and used it to haul the soldier out and over the side. He kept the gun. Barnabas pulled out the clip and slammed the gun down through the porthole. Screams and thuds answered the blow.

Behold the Queen's Rangers. So graceful. So dignified.

Listen. I am not going to take these insults from—ow!

Branch?

Bullet. Barnabas flexed his shoulder and hissed. The wound had barely broken the coat's fabric—some of the best tech to come out of Jean's labs—but there was going to be one hell of a bruise.

He reached down into the mech as it fired and bared his teeth at the first soldier he hauled up. "Turn this thing off."

"Don't do it!" the soldier cried dramatically. "Save yourself! Keep firing! For—"

"Look, if you're determined to die dramatically..." Barnabas held up the soldier's body as the mechs behind them started to fire, having finally noticed him.

The Yennai armor was not quite good enough for the soldier to survive that many direct hits, but both layers of it combined with the soldier's body were enough to keep Barnabas safe, at least.

"Thank you." Barnabas dumped the body off the side and jumped down into the interior before another round of bullets could reach him.

The mech pilot had his sidearm out, clutched in shaking hands. "I'm armed, and I warn you—we'll fight to the death!"

"That is just a ridiculous sentiment from someone who's trying to slaughter civilians," Barnabas informed him. "However, since you're all so damned insistent on this, I will help you out." He slashed the pilot's throat with one of his knives, turning the body, so the blood sprayed onto the back wall of the mech. "All right, how do I pilot this thing?"

There's probably a manual somewhere. Or, if you're determined to be manly, I can just let you figure it out on your own.

Some pointers would be helpful!

The joystick on the left will deviate you from the pre-set course and the joystick on the right is part of the point-and-shoot display. Also, the body can swivel on the base.

Excellent. How do I do that? I want to shoot at the rest of them.

Probably wise. They're arming missiles. I'd try the toggle switch above your head.

Doubtfully, Barnabas complied—only for the mech's body to do a dizzying 360-degree spin. He toggled it a bit more carefully the second time and wound up facing the other mechs.

They've been firing at you this whole time, but their bullets aren't very useful against the mech body. I'd suggest the missiles. They seem to be saving theirs for a special occasion.

What better occasion than this? Barnabas asked whimsically. He targeted another mech, pressed what he guessed was the missile launch button, and was rewarded by four missiles launching from the right side of the mech. It rocked on its spider feet, and the target exploded in a shower of sparks and splintering trees. *We probably didn't need all four of those.*

Probably not, no. Look down at the control panel for a moment? Okay, try the green button. Now the blue. Now press the blue and the orange at the same time while targeting that cluster of mechs over there. Whooooo!

We've started a forest fire.

We'll deal with that in a moment. Right now, you need to be anywhere but inside that mech.

Barnabas hauled himself out with a curse and tumbled into the undergrowth as several missiles slammed into the mech and knocked it back into a tree.

Ruuuuuun, tiny squishy human!

Barnabas ran.

Several mech crews, apparently not aware of who or what he was, decided to take this opportunity to avenge their fellow mech pilots' deaths. They piled out of the mechs and ran for him.

Unbelievable. Inside the mechs, they had armor and missiles. Outside...

Barnabas snickered as he dove into a slide and took out several pilots at the ankles. They yelped as they fell, and Barnabas rolled back to his feet. A few were still standing. He drove a fist into one's face, pivoted to bash another with his elbow, and seized a third by the lapels and kneed him in the chest. Two shots took out the two on the ground still moving.

Can you get to the center of town?

Yes, why?

Because there are two more Yennai carriers on the way, and I'm guessing it's nuke o'clock.

Barnabas turned and sprinted for the town. *Get word to the Jotun!*

They know. They're evacuating the troops and sending shuttles into the town. The *Shinigami* screamed overhead and banked sharply before descending. *I'm picking up as many as I can.*

I'll meet you there. Barnabas pushed himself as fast as he could, screaming for the Jotuns on the city walls to get to the center of town.

Koel Yennai had *wanted* to take this colony with infantry. No doubt he wanted an occupation, with the civilians held hostage for the Jotun Navy's good behavior.

But he'd been prepared for it to go wrong, and he was willing to sacrifice his own soldiers to make that happen.

Above Abassi, Commander Jeqwar swung her ship around and primed her missiles. All she had to do was intercept enough nukes for the evacuation to take place. After the last battle, she had no faith that she could take down a carrier.

"Do whatever you have to do," she told her fighter pilots as she launched them out into space.

"Yes, ma'am." They knew what that meant.

Nukes launched from the carriers, and Jeqwar let instinct take over. She directed her own missiles to intercept, keeping the destroyer in constant motion. Not a single one of the destroyers could afford to be taken down, not when they were all that stood between the nukes and the colony. They had arrived the fastest and now...

"All clear," came the transmission from the ground. "Get out of there. Don't wait, and don't engage." There was a pause, and the admiral added, "We can't fight this fleet."

21

A dmiral Threton was one of the most distinguished
officers the Jotun Navy had ever produced. A living
legend, he had single-handedly rescued several civilian
ships from a slaver attack back when he was just a
destroyer captain. Since that time, he had managed the
fleet through several engagements and war drills.

The problem was, Barnabas couldn't for the life of him
figure out which of the Jotuns standing on *Shinigami*'s
bridge before him was Admiral Threton.

"Help me," Barnabas said to Gar silently.

"How?"

"You introduce me as our emissary, and hopefully, their
second-in-command will introduce him."

"Clever," Shinigami commented. "Maybe you should
introduce *me* as our emissary, however."

"You can't project an avatar out here."

"Give me a body, then."

Barnabas refrained from rolling his eyes as Gar stepped

forward with a bow, gestured, and announced, "Barnabas, captain of the *Shinigami*."

Barnabas nodded to the group of three Jotun.

"Barnabas, this is Admiral Threton." The leftmost Jotun gestured to the one on the far right. "I am Commander Jeqwar, and this is Commander Celwar."

"I am pleased to meet you." Barnabas nodded to each of them in turn. "This is Venfaldri Gar, and my associate, Shinigami, is listening in remotely."

"Shinigami is an Artificial Intelligence, yes?" Admiral Threton sounded dubious. "Is it capable of drawing conclusions?"

"I assure you, aside from multitasking processing capabilities—in which capacity she far exceeds any of us—she is quite similar to any organic mind." Barnabas gestured to the ship. "She will be able to use the ship's external speakers to communicate with us."

Not that I intend to after that insult. "Is it capable of drawing conclusions?" What does he think I am, a pocket calculator?

Quick! 4 + 6.

I hate you.

Barnabas hid a smile. "We have important matters to discuss. Namely, how we intend to defeat the Yennai Corporation."

There was an awkward moment of silence, then the admiral made a noise Barnabas could only describe as clearing a mechanical throat.

Thankfully, he did not beat around the bush. "We aren't prepared to attack until we can be sure that we understand their cloaking and shield mechanisms," he said bluntly. "And we don't know when that will be."

"I'll help," Shinigami said. "We all need to know that. After all," she added smoothly, "we're on the clock now."

The Jotuns looked at one another.

Shinigami continued with only the faintest edge to her voice. "I assume we all understand that any appeasement efforts will be entirely useless. What Koel Yennai wants—"

"Is to rule this sector," the admiral interrupted. "We are aware of that, Miss Shinigami. At this point, we have to weigh his goals against his apparent desire to kill our entire populace if he does not get what he wants. Because it seems he can carry that plan out quite successfully."

"That would be short-sighted." Barnabas picked up the thread Shinigami had started. "Koel only wants you to believe the choices are between benevolent dictatorship and certain death. In fact, neither of those options are a true representation of the facts. He is using brutality to blind you."

"I am aware of his tactics, thank you." The admiral sounded unimpressed. "And I hold this position with the express purpose of defending my people. If I undertake a course of action which will result in deaths—perhaps thousands of deaths—I must be willing to say that it was truly the only way. I must be able to say with certainty that I *knew* more would die. Not that I simply believed Koel would eventually turn into a dictator."

"Idiot," Shinigami muttered over their comm.

"Hold on a moment."

Barnabas looked at the admiral. "What do you see as an alternative to an attack?"

"A false capitulation that sets him off his guard, followed by an attack at an appropriate time."

Barnabas nodded slowly. "And you think this has a chance of winning? You think Koel will not anticipate this, demand the imprisonment of your officer corps, and install some method of insurance in every Jotun colony?"

There was a long silence.

"You're right. He's an idiot."

"I do have some sympathy, though," Gar commented. "It would be a hard sell to go back and explain that he knew Koel was going to destroy colonies if he didn't back down...and he didn't back down."

"Then he just needs to take Koel out before Koel can take out any more colonies," Shinigami said promptly.

"Precisely," Barnabas agreed.

"Oh. I hadn't thought of that." Gar looked a little bewildered. "Why isn't he doing that?"

"He thinks the odds are too much of a long shot," Shinigami explained. To the admiral, she said, "We understand your desire to save as many lives as possible."

"We also respect your wish to make this a battle of wits as well as weapons," Barnabas added.

"The only way to win against Koel now, however," Shinigami finished, "is to hit him hard and fast and end his hopes entirely."

"That's easy for you to say," the admiral snapped. "*Your* colonies aren't in the crossfire."

"*Yet.*" Barnabas felt his lip curl in contempt, though he tried not to be too obvious about it. "I am not sure about Jotun history, but in *human* history, it is quite clear that when someone like Koel takes power, no one is safe. If we allow Koel's reach to grow longer, he *will* come for human colonies."

"Then summon your fleets to deal with him!"

"If we must, we will." Barnabas did not waver. "I am telling you, however, that we do not have time to get all of those ships here, and pulling them away from their current engagements will hurt us as well. I do not ask your ships to engage for no reason."

"Besides which, it's hardly unfair of us to ask you to fight Koel yourself when it's your colonies he's attacking at present," Gar pointed out.

"A very good point," Shinigami said over the comm.

"Thank you. Now, try not to roll your eyes too much. Just let me try something."

"All right," Barnabas said apprehensively.

"I'm intrigued," Shinigami said.

"With your politicians having sold out to the Yennai Corporation, this is a uniquely difficult operation for you," Gar observed.

Admiral Threton bristled at this. "We are hardly the only species that has had politicians taking bribes."

"That's not what I meant." Gar's voice rose slightly, but he got himself back under control. "You're quite correct. All species are corruptible, and Koel is very good at finding leverage. What I meant was that you are fighting, knowing that there is misinformation being spread, and knowing that your sacrifices are not being honored. That is...well, I cannot imagine how difficult it is. I know only the smallest part of that."

Admiral Threton looked at him curiously.

"I am Luvendi," Gar said with a shrug. "My family does not respect my choice to leave Luvendan. Though I have found great purpose and done many things of which I am proud, I know they think I shamed our family by leaving. I cannot imagine how much worse it must be to know that I would face imprisonment or disgrace, as you are."

"Er, Gar? Are you sure you're making this better?"

"Keep listening." Gar's subvocalization sounded serene.

The Jotuns looked at one another.

"You *know*," Gar said emphatically, "that they're back on Jotuna, making speeches and media statements, saying that you were supposed to be in prison, that you've brought the wrath of the Yennai Corporation down on the civilians… and they're just hoping, praying, that they'll make it out with their mansions and their bribes still intact."

Commander Jeqwar fairly growled her contempt. "Soft-living idiots. They do nothing for us. They sold us out to the Yennai. They gave them windows into our technology! They should be strung up for this."

Gar laughed. "But did you hear their communications when they arrived and saw your fleet? We caught a few pieces of chatter. They were flabbergasted. Whatever those politicians gave them, the Yennai fleet didn't have any idea they should expect you all. Oh, it was beautiful."

The Jotuns started to laugh as well, little mechanical chuckles.

I'll be damned, he's actually pulling it off. Barnabas saw where Gar was going with this, but he didn't want to intervene or even chime in. Gar had wormed his way into their good graces and was working them. Barnabas might only scare them off.

"They've handed so much over, though." Gar shook his head. "Like you said—the technology, the channels into the fleet. You managed to cut off their access, but that hardly excuses it. Those politicians thought they were giving all of that information up."

The Jotuns nodded.

"And right now…" Gar sounded thoughtful now. "I can't imagine what Koel is offering in bribes."

The Jotuns murmured to one another in alarm.

"You shut them out once," Gar said. "But any time they have, they can probably use to their advantage. Who knows what tricks they have up their sleeves now?"

"Treasonous bastards," the admiral rumbled. "We need time. We need to figure out where they're going, how their cloaking works, how those damned impervious *shields* of theirs work, and we have no such time."

"There's only one thing to do," Shinigami said simply. "We need to get one of their ships and use it."

A good point. Barnabas nodded slightly to himself. *If they've got any human colonies in their sights…*

Exactly.

"It would need to be a carrier," Commander Jeqwar said. "Or the *Avaris.* And that's a damned risky mission."

"We wouldn't want to send any more ships than we absolutely had to," Shinigami proposed. "Just us, I would think."

"I'll go as well." Jeltor, who had been in close conversation with another Jotun, clanked over and ducked his mechanical body to the admiral. "My actions at their headquarters were part of what got us into this mess. I can help fix it now."

"You fought back after they kidnapped you," the

admiral rumbled. "What were you supposed to do? Hell, what were *any* of us supposed to do—stand aside while our politicians sold us out and frolicked in their cash?"

Barnabas saw Gar's faint smile. The Luvendi's plan had been successful. By reminding them just how stacked the odds were, and *why* they were so stacked, he had lit a fire under the Jotun officers.

It was genius.

"They'll pay," Barnabas assured the admiral. "We'll make sure every piece of incriminating evidence we need appears in your media. They won't be able to keep people from knowing what they did. When this is over, they'll hang."

The admiral nodded decisively. "Good. Now, what do you need, to find that ship?"

"Anything you have that narrows down their location," Shinigami said. "We know they must have a patch of fairly empty space because we've never figured out where their shipyards are, and with so much cargo going from place to place...a few more shipments of steel and electronics don't stand out."

"We have a guess of where they are now." The admiral pressed a button on his suit. "Fretor, this is Admiral Threton. Send the possible location of the Yennai fleet to the *Shinigami*. Yes, I'm sure. Yes, it's me. Do it now." He turned back to the group. "I certainly hope you can do this quickly," he told them. "I have a feeling we don't have much time."

"Agreed," Barnabas said solemnly. "We'll do what we can and do it quickly—and then strike together. Wait for our signal. We may need you sooner rather than later."

"We'll be on alert. And...you were right." The admiral shook his head. "Whatever we give Koel, whether it's time or resources, he'll use it against us. We have to strike soon."

22

For two days, the *Julentai* hung in a field of rubble around a comet and waited while Chofal and Dretkalor camped out in the cockpit and assessed each ship that passed.

They dismissed so many that Zinqued began to have fantasies of firing them both. First, a ship was too small, then too old, then too large, then too new.

"Too *new?*" Zinqued demanded. If he had any hair, he'd have been pulling it out at that point. As it was, he was very tempted to stab himself in the eye just to make a distraction from all this insanity.

Dretkalor and Chofal looked at one another.

"Yes," Dretkalor said finally as if explaining something to a very stupid toddler. "The *Julentai* is old and has very old components. If we try to add something that's too new, it might break everything. The voltage standards have changed, among other things."

Zinqued suppressed a shriek and stormed off to find

out if any of the new guards had figured out how to distill alcohol. He could use a drink.

He was exceedingly surprised, therefore, when there was a shout from the bridge and Dretkalor sprinted down the hall in the middle of dinner to announce that they'd found it, they'd found the ship they needed, and everyone needed to get ready to fight.

"I assume you don't mean me," Tik'ta said acidly. She had gotten progressively more and more annoyed at being shut off the bridge of her ship, and nothing Zinqued said about taking a vacation seemed to make an impact.

She stomped off to the cockpit while Dretkalor waved the rest of them out of the room.

"I can't even finish my food?" Zinqued asked, annoyed. They *would* decide to attack now, those two. It just *had* to be during dinner.

He would remember this when it came time to give out yearly bonuses.

He muttered to himself the whole time he suited up in his armor and weapons. When he returned to the cockpit, Tik'ta had begun to warm up the engines and their prey was just in sight.

Chofal and Dretkalor both laughed, but Zinqued swore. "That? *That's* the ship you're going to steal from?"

"*Yes,*" the two of them said in unison.

"It's a bucket of bolts," Zinqued said dangerously.

"Look at the engines," Chofal pointed out. "You only get that greenish tint from hyperwave propulsion. They tried to mask it, but once you know what to scan for, you can see they've got a good ship under there."

"And there," Dretkalor added. "They've put false plating over the hull."

"And *that's* not too new?" Zinqued was grumpy. He should have seen all of that. In fact, if he'd been a little less hasty, he would have. Now he looked like an idiot in front of his new crew.

"Most of the hyperwave propulsion ships were built years ago and upgraded," Chofal explained. "Their parts are very adaptable." She smiled, looking almost wistful. "This is a jackpot. I could work on it for weeks. If we stripped off its power couplings—"

"Chofal, focus. Have you forgotten that we're going to be stealing a much better ship than this one?"

"Oh!" She brightened visibly. "Right. Just wait till you see that one," she confided in Dretkalor. "Absolutely beautiful. Just gorgeous. Every system—"

"All right, everyone except Zinqued *off my bridge*," Tik'ta snapped. "Go wax poetically about dream ships somewhere else."

Everyone else shuffled out. Chofal was too engaged in her monologue even to be shamed. They heard her chattering all the way to her bunk to pick up her tools and her spacesuit.

Tik'ta rolled her eyes. "Neither of them ever stops talking, do they?"

"That's enough," Zinqued admonished. It seemed like the sort of thing a captain would say. He didn't want any ill feeling to spring up between his crew.

Tik'ta sighed, but as their target drew closer, she needed to focus on that. Over the past few days, she had needed to learn the systems on the *Julentai* and hadn't gotten the time she needed in the cockpit to learn them.

Nevertheless, she had piloted similar ships. As their target passed by, she lifted the *Julentai* away from a piece of rock, flipped it, and slid under the other ship.

There were many subtle and highly technical ways to steal a ship. The *Julentai* had none of them. What it did have was a broadwave transmitter that flooded all the ship's channels with random data, an EMP pulse that knocked out the systems and allowed the *Julentai* to take hold of them, and multiple clamps that held the ship in place.

Tik'ta gave a triumphant grin as she worked on the controls of the other ship. "Got it. They're trying to get the engines back, though—get on board and stop them before they fly us back into the comet."

"Radio if you need anything." Zinqued took off and made for the small bay on the bottom of the ship.

It was an ingenious little design. An airtight compartment at the corner of the docking bay held a second airtight compartment that would slide down out of the belly of the ship, leaving a vacuum behind it. The air from the inner compartment was vented into the first, the inner compartment resealed, then opened into space. No precious air was lost, and the ship was safe from any breach.

In the silence, the crew fired a cable down to the hull of the captured ship, attached themselves to it, and pushed off gently to slide along and cluster at the end.

There was a similar compartment in this ship, and

Chofal took the lead on opening it. She had to hotwire one of the panels in the end, and even then, it took two of the Brakalons to haul it open. Having braced themselves against the hull, they floated up.

This was why they strapped themselves to the cable. It was all too easy to lose your footing at a time like this and wind up too close to the engines. Zinqued shuddered.

He had heard stories he didn't particularly want to remember, but each one was seared into his brain.

They heard scuffling outside the compartment as they locked themselves into it and depressurized. They had to secure themselves with clamps because once they passed the hull, the internal grav systems kicked in. Nevertheless, they got the floor closed and their weapons raised.

"Tik'ta, broadcast the message."

"Yes, sir." She allowed it through on their suits' channel as well:

"This is the captain of the *Julentai*. We require two components of your ship. Your crew will not be hurt if they do not interfere. Your ship will not be vented, nor will it be rendered inoperable."

There was shouting. Zinqued pressed the button to open the door, and he and the four Brakalons rushed out and took cover, scanning the area with their weapons.

The crew in the landing bay had decided to take his advice. They had their weapons on the floor and their hands up. One of the Brakalons collected their weapons and secured their hands behind their heads, and the other four guided Chofal toward the engineering bay. The booster would be there.

The first attack came when they'd almost reached the engine room. A crazed Leath jumped out from one of the side corridors, brandishing a gun and screaming. He opened fire as one of the Brakalons tackled Chofal to the ground to shield her. The rest of them fired and their attacker crumpled to the ground.

The captain waited for them in the engine room, much more sensibly pointing his gun toward the reactor itself.

Everyone stopped. If the reactor were open, the captain would be dying quickly. If it were closed, which it appeared to be, it was unlikely that a bullet could pierce the casing. Unlikely…

But not impossible.

"I won't let you leave us out here to drift!" The captain's voice was wild.

"You won't be left to drift," Zinqued said as soothingly as he could. He didn't have any particular desire to die from radiation poisoning. "Our engineer needs your zero-point booster and your fruit bowl."

He pointed to the auxiliary photonic dish to make it clear what he meant. Though it was a precisely made and highly technical piece of equipment, it resembled a dish for fruit. It could be a bowl for anything, of course, but somehow the name had stuck.

Paun had once told Zinqued that you could tell a good engineer by which technical terms they *didn't* use. "And don't trust any 'engineer' who calls that an auxiliary photonic dish," he finished.

That litmus test had served Zinqued well as he searched for a backup engineer for Chofal.

The captain narrowed his eyes at them, and Dretkalor

raised his rifle. His finger was conspicuously off the trigger.

"You shoot our mechanic," he said, "or that reactor, I shoot you. You don't shoot anything, I *don't* shoot you. You got that?"

The captain hesitated, but at last he nodded, and Zinqued waved Chofal into the engine room.

She worked cheerfully, chattering about the specifications of the ship—not so much to them as to herself. Not that they all understood much anyway. She didn't seem to need answers, so the rest of them ignored her and kept their guns up, listening closely for anyone trying to sneak up on them.

Defeated, the captain went to sit in the corner. He still had his gun, but he wasn't pointing it at the reactor anymore.

"Got it," Chofal said finally.

"Let's move," Zinqued ordered.

They left quickly, Dretkalor's gun still trained on the captain. The parts they had stolen were worth thousands, but true to their word—the ship would fly just fine.

They got back through the halls with no surprises and collected the guard they had left behind in the landing bay. One crew member was laid out with a split lip. No one mentioned anything about it as they crowded into the airlock chamber again, though the guard took one of the guns that had been surrendered, a particularly nice sniper rifle.

Zinqued didn't mention anything about that. Their business was stealing, after all, and a crew that could get little things they liked was a crew that was less likely to mutiny.

Their return to the *Julentai* was uneventful, and Tik'ta informed them the engines on their captive ship would not fire properly for two hours after they left, giving them plenty of time to escape.

"They aren't associated with any particular government," she said. "If they had powerful friends, I think they would have made that clear. They're probably *gori*."

"What are *gori*?" Dretkalor asked, with a frown.

"So there's something you don't know?" Tik'ta arched a brow. At Zinqued's look, however, she didn't press it further and just sighed. "It's a Torcellan word. They're… high-class couriers, I guess you could say. Merchants will use them as go-betweens and entrust them with…well, messages, usually."

"They weren't very keen to fight." Dretkalor scoffed.

"They probably didn't have a message on board. And those stealth systems take some serious money to run. If they're being paid, they're probably running entirely dark." She shrugged. "Maybe they worked for the Yennai Corporation, back when money was still flowing."

"There's going to be a lot to harvest when they finally fall apart." Zinqued smiled at the thought.

"I wouldn't count them out," Tik'ta warned him.

"She's right," Dretkalor agreed. "Everyone who's met Mr. Yennai says he never gives up. Never."

Tik'ta looked pleased that Dretkalor had agreed with her. "See?" she asked Zinqued.

Zinqued shook his head. "What does he have left to

fight for? His children are dead, he'll have no one to take over after him."

"Someone like him only ever wants one thing." Tik'ta looked at him meaningfully. "*More.*"

She turned back to her work and left Zinqued to go back to the engine room, frowning. Tik'ta had been spouting a platitude, nothing more.

So why had he felt a chill when he heard those words?

23

"It's known to run supplies into this sector," argued one of the officers. "And it would make a good warning shot against the humans."

Everyone glanced over to where Koel sat enigmatically in his throne-like chair.

Lotar knew just what Koel was doing. He had, most likely, already picked what he thought was the best position. However, to keep his officers from agreeing with him out of habit and to see which of them would come up with the solution he liked best—not to mention, to see if any of them would come up with a better solution—he kept his opinions on the matter to himself.

It was a smart thing for him to do. Unfortunately, just because Lotar knew what he was doing and why didn't make it any less scary.

And he knew that Koel was waiting for him to say something. It had become clear over the past few days that Koel viewed him as a protege...or potential protege.

Lotar just had to prove himself.

NATALIE GREY & MICHAEL ANDERLE

The problem was that he was sure he knew what Koel wanted to hear, and he was terrified to say it. It was an effective tactic, but it was a cruel one, and he was afraid that Koel would actually take the suggestion if Lotar made it.

Then Lotar would feel guilty. The thought of the operation made him want to cry.

He faced the bleak possibility of saying nothing. It would take little for Koel to grow tired of him and shuffle him off to some minor ship. Lotar was sure he could deal with the whispers and the stares: *poor bastard, he disappointed Mr. Yennai. At least he's still alive, anyway.* But the thought of disappointing Koel distressed him. There was something about the Torcellan, something almost hypnotic. You looked into his eyes, and you wanted to do anything, say anything, to please him.

Which meant that Lotar wanted more than anything to give the suggestion that was on the tip of his tongue.

"We don't have good enough human targets yet," the admiral said. "We continue to apply pressure to the Jotun. Once they're forced by their government to pull back, we have one less enemy. We can decide what to do about the humans at our leisure rather than striking out randomly."

It was a much better suggestion than attacking the human cargo ships. Lotar found himself nodding.

And yet...

He bit his lip. He didn't want to say this. He could just picture what would to happen if he did.

"Mr. Venn." Koel did not raise his voice, but everyone swiveled to Lotar. "Did you have a suggestion to make?"

Lotar froze. The other officers looked at him with poorly-concealed distaste.

He could do this. He just had to survive Koel's disappointment.

"I like the admiral's suggestion," Lotar said honestly. "Forcing the Jotuns to break their alliance with the human means that we can divide their forces more equally."

The admiral gave a confident smile. Even Koel's new protege liked his plan.

Koel said nothing. He looked at Lotar, and he waited.

"Or we could strike the planet Devon." The words were dragged out of Lotar's chest. He couldn't hold them back.

Koel smiled thinly in triumph.

"Devon?" the admiral repeated. "Where is that?"

"It's not in this sector, sir." Lotar felt himself moving toward the table as if in a dream. He had said it. He had to follow through now. He brought up the reports he had written after combing through the *Shinigami's* data banks. "It used to be known as Devon and is now called High Tortuga by the humans. They've made several very clumsy attempts to hide it."

The admiral blinked.

"What we've seen of their warning systems *is* impressive," Lotar admitted. "It's all second-hand, but most of the merchants who are usually able to get onto planets to supply black markets, cannot this time."

He snuck a glance. Koel's eyebrows had gone up at that. Lotar knew that Koel held the deepest respect for black markets, believing them to be a nearly infallible mechanism for breaking down any restrictions on trade.

Usually, he was right. In this case, the humans had managed to keep a lock-down on the planet.

"The humans were responsible for the destruction of some Yennai-affiliated groups on Devon," Lotar continued. "They were working as mercenaries on the less populous continent. Apparently, the humans took exception to that. The details aren't entirely clear."

"Someone must know them," Koel interjected.

Everyone else exchanged glances. He'd started to get impatient, and they were eager to see Lotar taken down a notch or two. No one liked the way they had squabbled without Koel saying a word, only for Lotar to speak up late and get all the credit.

I wish any of you were in my place, Lotar wanted to say. But it wasn't really true—he'd be jealous if anyone else were to take Koel's attention and win his respect.

"Another mercenary syndicate did know what happened," Lotar explained. "At least, as far as I can tell, they did. They appear to have sent reinforcements."

"Appear to have sent? Did you contact them?"

Lotar swallowed. "They're all dead. Sir," he added.

Koel thought that over, his eyes shifted to the darkness outside the windows. He seemed calm.

Then Koel said, not even raising his voice, "So the humans destroyed our affiliates. They sought out any of their contacts and destroyed those as well. Then they tracked those contacts to our headquarters and killed both of my children."

The stateroom was entirely silent. No one, not even Lotar, spoke. Shoulders were hunched. Everyone tried desperately to disappear.

Koel stood and swept down the stairs. He looked at the reports projected on the table, his gaze ravenous.

"Uleq was right," he said, almost to himself. "I did not listen when he told me how dangerous they were. I thought we could infiltrate them when the time came." He looked up at Lotar. "You understand?"

Everyone else now looked grateful that they were not on the spot, and Lotar struggled to figure out what Koel meant.

"We must destroy them?"

"Yes," Koel said. "But more than that, Lotar, we must admit our mistakes. The game of power is unforgiving. There is little room for errors, and no room to cling to them. I disregarded Uleq's warnings. It cost me both my children." His fingers tightened on the edge of the table. "I will not make the same mistake twice. When we go to Devon, we will go in force, and we will make the planet a barren husk. Before the fires have even died, we will find every human colony there is and destroy it. I wanted to make an example for the humans." Now his eyes swept the room. "I see that is too dangerous. We will kill them, every one of them."

He left the table without another glance, headed for the door, and from somewhere, the admiral drummed up the courage to call after him.

"Sir, what do we do about the Jotun fleet for now?"

Koel paused. The admiral shook.

Koel did not even look back. "Let them discover on their own that we will be at Devon. Make them think it is a small detachment of our fleet. We will crush them both at once."

NATALIE GREY & MICHAEL ANDERLE

"Got it!" Chofal grinned as the device powered up. "And we're good to go. Look at this beauty." She jerked her head at Dretkalor. "Come on, teach it what it needs to know."

"It's not a pet." But the Brakalon obliged, coming to sit in front of the device. He moved carefully to enter the various codes.

"Do you think it'll work?" Chofal asked anxiously.

"Better hope so." Dretkalor grinned. "Zinqued paid out the ass for them. Plus," he added thoughtfully, "we'll be a cloud of dust if they don't."

Chofal chewed her lip. But the *Shinigami* swam before her eyes, perfect and gleaming. Those engines, that electrical grid…

She had to get her hands on it.

"Come on," she said to Dretkalor. "Let's go tell Zinqued we're done. He and Tik'ta were looking for the Yennai fleet. We can finally set a course to meet up with them."

It's worth noting, Shinigami said acidly, *that we don't even know what other ships are around us. Even I didn't know that destroyer was there. And we don't know how this one jumps around without gates.*

I'm willing to bet that's actually a set of decoy signals, Barnabas said. He'd been thinking a lot about this. *I mean, we know they do this differently than we do. Differently even than the Jotun do. So I'm thinking perhaps in their systems, you employ a sudden cloaking technique, visual-based, and you just accelerate damned fast so that no one has a chance to crack the scanner cloaking before they realize where you've gone.*

That's a damned lot of effort to go to for a trick.

Hardly a trick. If you can convince people you're gone, they generally stop shooting.

What I'm getting from this is, never stop shooting.

That's the one. Barnabas snapped his helmet into place. *Are we in place yet?*

Close. For the better part of two hours, Shinigami had approached the *Avaris*, sliding slowly and inexorably through the fleet.

In their last engagements, and from the hacking she had experienced at their hands, she had theorized that the ships networked with one another to build a much more accurate grid of any known enemies. It was the smart way to do things, and Koel had been consistently and infuriatingly intelligent about all of this.

What all of this meant was that Shinigami had to be very, very careful to send signals to any ship that might sense her on its scanners. As the ships changed formation even while the fleet was in stasis, that had been a slow process.

She had managed it, however. Barnabas had told her that infiltration was more a game of patience than anything else, and that advice had proved invaluable. Together, they tracked fighter patrols and watched the formations changing, and now they were here.

She guessed Barnabas' thoughts. *You want to go down there and kill him, don't you?*

Yes, Barnabas admitted. *Cutting the head off the snake isn't always the answer, but he's always been instrumental in holding this together. If we could take him and his top level out, a lot of it would be over.*

Shinigami waited for him to say that he wouldn't do it and eventually got worried. She peered through the cameras to find him climbing down the ladder toward the surface of the *Avaris*.

Barnabas. You know you can't get through that many people on your own, right?

I know. His voice was subdued. *I promised no heroics. It would kill both of us—and Tafa, and Gar, and Jeltor. And if we failed, there would be no one left who knew what was coming or had our ideas of how to stop it.*

Shinigami said nothing.

It's just difficult, Barnabas confessed finally. He paused as he helped Jeltor down onto the top of the ship. The two of them set off, two tiny figures on the top of the dreadnought. *The temptation is always to go in directly and—we're going in the correct direction, right?*

Yes, Shinigami said, amused. *I'll mark the location on your helmet display.*

Oh. I see it, yes. Like I was saying, the temptation is to go in directly. Finish it all. Believe it or not, I understood what the admiral was saying. Taking the time to make a good plan is difficult when you know innocent people might die in the meantime.

More innocent people die in the end if you do things the stupid way.

I know that. It's a train-tracks problem, though.

What?

If you can direct the train to kill fewer people, but... You know what, not important. Suffice it to say, you are entirely

*correct from a logical standpoint, but emotions are by definition
not logical.*

*Scarily accurate. All right, you're getting close. Set the
crawler down?*

Barnabas knelt and released a tiny, spidery-looking
robot. It skittered up to something that looked rather like
an open porthole and climbed inside.

"Come back now," Shinigami told them.

"Did we really need to come here to do this?" Jeltor
asked.

"Probably not, but you really seemed to want to help.
Besides which, shooting a small robot at a dreadnought
while both of them are traveling several thousand kilome-
ters per hour seems like it has the potential to go wrong.
Just saying."

Barnabas snickered.

Picturing it?

Yep. He let Jeltor go up the ladder first. *Are you getting
any data yet?*

*No, but be patient. It won't be long. We just have to hang here
for a few hours—*

In the middle of an enemy fleet.

*Yes, that. Eventually, that little bugger will reach something
useful. For now, I'm going to focus on making sure it doesn't trip
any security systems. I'll tell you when there's news.*

Back in the hold, Barnabas stripped off his spacesuit
and gave a regretful look at the reflection of his hair in the
visor. He looked at Jeltor. "You're lucky you don't need a
spacesuit."

"I have to travel in a vat of water. I'm always in a
spacesuit."

"That's a good point." Barnabas set off for the kitchen. "We should find something to do for a few hours, until—"

He was interrupted by the sound of mechanical laughter.

"Shinigami?"

It was a few moments before Shinigami recovered enough to talk. "Oh, you are not going to believe this." She was still cackling. "You are not going to *believe* this. Oh, this is priceless. They're going to attack High Tortuga."

"Which, if you'll recall, was our greatest fear."

"Uh-huh. Just come into the conference room, and I'll show you their battle plan, though." She was still laughing. "I can't wait to show the Jotun fleet *this*. This is amazing. I'm going to see if I can get that crawler onto the bridge so I can see their faces when we get there and they see where they are."

24

"She's sure they've fucked up that badly?" Gar asked a while later. He sounded doubtful. He swung his arms to loosen them and watched as Barnabas warmed up.

At the edge of the room, beyond the mats, Jeltor watched curiously. Jotun tended to be a fairly insular species, and their reliance on powersuits meant any physical altercation could be fatal.

They could sling insults with the best of them, but they did not have physical fights.

Which was just as well, really, Jeltor thought now. When bipedal aliens fought, there was a certain grace to it. They could contort their bodies, and they could summon great power.

When two Jotun fought—as children sometimes did—it was just two bags of jelly slapping each other with thin, noodle-like tentacles. Not dignified. Not even impressive. Just sad.

Jeltor was, therefore, intrigued by Barnabas and Gar's sparring.

"She's very sure," Barnabas said. "I made her stay to double-check. They have the battle plan, and they've 'leaked' information to the Jotuns to try to get them there as well. I'll tell you, I had a hell of a time trying to get Admiral Threton to walk right into the trap."

"It's hard to blame him for that," Jeltor said, scrupulously accurate. Admiral Threton had plenty of faults, to be sure, but this wasn't one of them.

"Oh, I know that. But we know a lot more now. We *know* Koel's plan."

Barnabas continued to speak as he slid into motion. It happened so gracefully, in fact, that Jeltor hardly noticed it. He only realized what he saw a split-second before Gar went flying and slid into the wall. Barnabas wore a slight smile, lips curving in genuine amusement.

Jeltor saw the logic of it. The fight didn't start when Gar was ready. One could never expect a fight to start predictably.

Barnabas charged for another attack, but Gar seemed to have taken the lesson to heart. He dove sideways at the last second and threw up one leg for a grounded kick. Barnabas doubled over, narrowly avoiding a faceplant into the wall. Gar launched himself up and drove one fist into Barnabas' stomach.

Barnabas grunted in pain, but he didn't lose his focus. He wrenched Gar's fist before the Luvendi could withdraw it and used it to drag his opponent closer, directing a flurry of blows at Gar's relatively unprotected torso and head with his free hand.

Gar, not to be outdone, swept his foot behind Barnabas' even as the punches landed, and the two crashed onto the mats with a series of thuds that made Jeltor pulse in sympathetic pain.

They grappled, and their movement was so fast that Jeltor could hardly decipher the intricacies of it. He tried to assess it regarding their skeletal structure and musculature, but once he'd managed to understand how a particular move was made, he had invariably missed a few others that were just as impressive.

"Shinigami, can you give me security footage of this later? Slowed way, way down?"

Shinigami projected herself into the room next to Jeltor. "Why?" she asked curiously.

"Because I don't understand any of it, but it's fascinating." Jeltor waved one mechanical hand at the proceedings. The two were circling one another again. "I'm beginning to think that Jotuns should learn to fight physically as a method of training for space battles."

"That's an interesting thought." Shinigami considered. "I can definitely get you the footage. It must be hard to break down into useful data. I can see why you're struggling if you don't have..." She gestured at her projected body. "You know, *limbs.*"

"I wish I could see how the nerve impulses are working," Jeltor said wistfully. "Where do the movements originate? How do the muscles contract?"

"Heads!"

Jeltor only just managed to get sideways in time as Barnabas and Gar hurtled into the wall at high speed, crashing through Shinigami's hologram. Both of them, Jeltor noted with amusement, hunched over to try not to smash into her too hard. Instinct was a powerful thing.

Shinigami also found it amusing. She cackled and projected herself hovering cross-legged over the center of the mats.

"Rude," she called down. "Make it up to me by fighting for my amusement."

Barnabas glared at her, which gave Gar a good opening to punch him in the face. Barnabas responded with a flurry of kicks. He laid his torso back and lashed out with his heel, the top of his foot, and finally—picking his torso up slightly—punched his foot forward to send Gar flying.

Barnabas recovered a little inelegantly.

"*Oof*," Gar grunted from the other side of the room. He pushed himself up with a woebegone look. "Just a moment. I need some water."

Barnabas nodded. He looked quietly smug, as Jeltor had noticed he often did when he had done something sneaky.

Shinigami cocked her head to the side. "I've finished up an analysis on the Yennai cloaking if you want to give it a look, Jeltor. Between the Jotuns' cloaking and what the Yennai ships seem to have, we should be able to secure a significant advantage in that battle."

"I like the sound of that." Jeltor nodded to Barnabas and Gar and clanked off down the hall.

"You kids play nice," Shinigami said before disappearing in a puff of smoke.

"Why the smoke?" Gar asked. He stared up at the space where she disappeared.

"It's how genies appear and disappear. With lamps."

"*Lamps?*"

"Yes, because you rub the lamp and… This is going to take a lot of explaining. Genies are magic spirits who hide inside everyday objects, such as an oil lamp, and can be summoned out. They appear in a puff of smoke." Barnabas looked at Gar's awestruck face and remembered the most important factor. "Also, they aren't real. It's a myth."

"*Oh.*" Gar rubbed his head. "I thought I was going mad."

"No, no," Barnabas assured him hastily. He started stretching again. "So, how have you been? There hasn't been much time to debrief since we encountered the Yennai Corporation and—"

Gar pushed himself up on his elbows. His eyes were narrowed. "Shinigami told you. Or was it Tafa?"

"I noticed you were a bit subdued," Barnabas admitted. "Shinigami mentioned you were processing some things."

"You could say that." Gar looked down at his hands. It was still incredible to him that he could use them as weapons. "I've been thinking a lot about what it means to be weak, and what it means to be strong."

Barnabas took a seat on a pile of mats, his brows raised.

"I hated weak people for a long time," Gar explained. "Myself included. Weak people were vulnerable. They needed to be protected. I didn't realize that I *should* hate the people who hurt them."

Barnabas waited.

"And then I realized that it didn't matter how I felt about any of it," Gar said finally. "I just had to do the right thing. That's been very...liberating."

Barnabas considered this, intrigued. "I hadn't thought of that," he admitted. "You don't have to feel any particular way, you simply have to do the right thing. I like that. I like it a lot."

Gar smiled. "You do the right things for the right reasons, though. Someday, I hope to do that."

To his surprise, Barnabas started laughing.

"You're giving me far, far too much credit," the man said. "Gar, you forget how old I am."

"*Old.*" Shinigami's voice echoed around the gym.

"Yes, thank you, Shinigami." He gave Gar a wry look. "She's right, you know. I've had centuries to make mistakes —and, most importantly, learn when not to say anything, so I appear mysterious and profound."

"*I KNEW IT.*"

"Don't you have military schematics to be discussing?"

"I'm doing that, too," Shinigami said airily. "I just wanted to say I totally called that. I knew you weren't all that wise."

"I have legitimately learned some things, you know."

"Uh-huh. Keep telling yourself that. You want some *real* talk, Gar? Every twenty-five years or so, sometimes less, most sentient species have a total crisis and wonder if they've messed up their lives."

"Really?" Gar looked intrigued. "I suppose that does track. So that just never gets better, then?"

"I'm afraid not. Be warned, though. Now that you're *here*, if you ever get excessively emo about it and start playing meaningful songs and cutting your hair differently—or whatever it is Luvendi do—I *will* mock you. I say this as a friend who cares about you. I will mock you. A lot."

"Thank you, Shinigami." Barnabas gave a wry smile at the speakers then looked back at Gar. "She has a point, however. I hope you don't take it too much to heart, all this turmoil. It's good to question what you're doing and why. It's not good to wallow in it."

"No wallowing. Right." Gar picked himself up. "How long do we have before we reach High Tortuga?"

"Not too long." Barnabas pulled his armor from a nearby cabinet.

"I thought this was going to be entirely a space battle," Gar said, confused.

"I prefer to wear armor anyway. It helps me…get in the mood." Barnabas smiled.

"Some men light candles and play jazz," Shinigami commented.

"Shinigami, if I ever do that before a battle, you have permission to smack me."

She chortled. "I'll remind you of that."

Tik'ta had nearly fallen asleep when the computer dinged loudly. She jerked, fell off her seat, and swore as she wound up on the floor in a clatter of scales.

She peeked up over the side of the desk, and her eyes widened.

"Zinqued!" She scrabbled for her radio and couldn't find it. She must have knocked it off the desk when she fell. She shouted down the hall that led to the living quarters. "Zinqued!"

She was typing in coordinates with a feverish intensity when he arrived, the rest of the crew at his heels.

"What is it?"

"I found them." Tik'ta gave him a sharp-toothed grin. "I

found the Yennai fleet, and they're not too far away. They're heading for battle now, and you're never going to *believe* where they're going."

The crew all looked at one another.

"Where?" Zinqued finally asked.

"*Devon*," Tik'ta announced. "That's where Barnabas first started out, and he's been hunting down everyone who knows where it is. I tried to find it, but they'd changed the records in every database I could get my hands on."

"Why did you want to go there?" Dretkalor asked.

"I wanted to know what was going on there," Tik'ta said. "If they're going to so much trouble to hide it…"

Everyone nodded.

"Anyway, the Yennai fleet discovered where it is, and they're on their way."

"It's going to be a smoking wreck by the time they're done with it," Dretkalor said.

"Yep." Tik'ta looked almost pleased. "Surrounded by a debris cloud full of Yennai ships, human ships, Jotun ships…"

In a flash, Zinqued realized where she was going with this. "We'll be getting a bigger haul than we expected."

"*Way* bigger." She looked incredibly pleased. "When the smoke clears, we're going to have the best ship in the sector—and plenty of tech we can sell."

Everyone's faces settled into looks of gleeful anticipation. The way Dretkalor's hands moved, he was dreaming about guns. Chofal gazed back at the engine room with a look of dreamy happiness on her face. Zinqued had closed his eyes, and Tik'ta guessed he was picturing himself on the bridge of a gleaming new ship.

"I'm laying in a course for the Yennai fleet," she told them all. "Get ready. We're now the crew of the Yennai frigate *Haron's Shield.*" She sighed. "I'm not sure we'll arrive before them, though. I hoped we would."

Zinqued laughed. He couldn't help it. He was giddy, and he couldn't picture anything bringing him down. "Maybe it'll be better to get there a little late," he pointed out. "We'll have an idea of how the battle's going, and any major surprises will already have happened."

"Good point." Tik'ta nodded. "You know, I did always want to see Devon. Guess that dream's down the toilet. I like this one better, though."

She swung back to her console and guided the ship to full acceleration.

Not long now, and they'd have everything they ever wanted.

25

Lotar had paced the junior officers' bunks for most of the day. The rest of them, caught between envy and anticipation, didn't waste much time on him. No one, it seemed, wanted to speak to him anymore.

He wished they would, but what was he going to say? He couldn't admit that he felt bad about what was going to happen.

They'd be only too glad to pass along to Koel that Lotar thought he was a mass-murdering psychopath.

If Lotar had just had the sense to keep his mouth shut, they'd be headed for the Jotun fleet, and all the civilians on Devon—or High Tortuga, or whatever the humans called it now—would be safe.

But he kept reliving the moment of Koel's happiness. When Lotar had given him a good suggestion, Koel had been quite pleased, indeed.

It still made Lotar shiver. He knew beyond a doubt that he would do the same thing again. It gave him a sick feeling in the pit of his stomach, but also the feeling of terrible *rightness*. He had always excelled at finding patterns.

Now he had found his place. Hadn't he?

When a bridge officer showed up in the doorway, everyone scurried out of his way, and Lotar tried to make himself look presentable. His hair was a mess. What if the bridge officer told Koel about that?

The bridge officer just sneered. "Mr. Yennai wants to see you at the ship's magazine," he relayed and disappeared before Lotar managed to ask where that even was.

In a ship this big, there was no good way to guess which level and sector one might find anything in. Lotar sighed, tried to make his hair presentable, and practically ran out the door. He paused and turned back to the other officers.

"I don't suppose any of you know where the magazine is."

They all shrugged, but then Era, to his surprise, elbowed another officer, a Torcellan female.

"Palla, you know. Tell him."

Palla looked far from pleased about Era's intervention, but she wasn't willing to lie outright. "Level 14, Sector 2," she told Lotar grudgingly. "You can get there faster if you take the mechanics' lifts."

"Thank you," Lotar said with feeling.

He arrived in the magazine still reeking of carbon and grease from the mechanics' lifts. As a pleasant surprise, the smell wasn't too noticeable compared to the munitions.

Koel and several of his officers were clustered around a tower of some sort, maybe three stories high with thick cables lining its sides. At the top were metal spikes, easily three feet long and serrated. Lotar gulped.

"Ah, Lotar." Koel beckoned him forward. "Come see this."

Lotar came closer, somewhat unwillingly. The cables filled him with a sort of dread, though he wasn't quite sure why. It was amazing how you didn't have to know *exactly* what a piece of technology was used for, to divine its larger purpose.

Koel stroked one of the cables, and Lotar had the sudden, hysterical urge to ask if the thing was alive.

Please no, please no, please no.

"This is the latest innovation from my laboratories," Koel said with a smile. "Isn't it beautiful? It latches on there, you see, and these arms can tear a ship to pieces. Then they weaponize the shards of it. Each arm is attached to an explosive chamber. They rip apart, seek other ships, and use the power of the arm to bash through the hull with the shards, and explode inside them."

It was such a visceral image that Lotar swallowed. "Very nice," he managed.

"We'll be at Devon soon. I want you on the bridge with me, Lotar. Your assessments of the Jotun fleet will be very useful."

Lotar, still staring at the missile, felt the sudden, desperate need to be anywhere else. He nodded his head so far, he practically bowed.

"I'll go gather my research on the Jotun fleet's capabilities, and will meet you on the bridge, Mr. Yennai."

"So this is High Tortuga." Jeltor stared out the bridge window of the *Shinigami*.

"Beautiful, isn't it?" Gar came to stand beside him. He pointed. "That's the main continent. Most of the note-worthy things happen over there, I'm given to understand. And that's the smaller continent. Barnabas calls it the Wild North."

"Wild West," Barnabas corrected with a smile. He was seated in the captain's chair and was reading printouts Shinigami had made for him. She sat in her usual chair, one leg draped over the arm, toying with a double-barreled pistol that seemed to have a wooden handle.

"Right, Wild West."

"Although Wild North does have a ring to it." Barnabas raised his eyebrows. "Driving snow… I'm picturing moun-tains. No, glaciers."

"Big fuckin' bears," Shinigami opined.

"What are bears?" Gar asked. Jeltor also looked curious.

"Oh, man." Shinigami sat up. "So, you know what tanks are, right? Yeah, so picture a tank covered in fur, with really big teeth."

Both aliens looked at her like they hoped she was joking.

"It's a fairly accurate summation," Barnabas agreed. "The other thing is that you never run from bears. They have no natural predators. You have to stand your ground, or they'll think you're prey."

Gar and Jeltor stood frozen.

"Never. Going. To Earth," Gar muttered.

Jeltor gave a mechanical nod.

Shinigami snickered. "So, how do things stand?"

"Shouldn't we be asking *you*? I thought you were the one with the built-in scanners."

"I was daydreaming." She sat up and cocked her head to the side. "The Jotuns are getting in formation. We have them running a scanning subroutine I found in the Yennai systems that might give us a chance at seeing any cloaked ships. Also, I've boosted our cloaking and theirs with a similar program to the one the Yennai use. I think."

"You think?"

"Computer systems for a fleet are...how do I put this delicately—"

"You've never put anything delicately in your life."

"Oh, right. That makes things easier, then. They're gigantic fucking monstrosities. The size of Chuck Norris's balls. Easy."

Barnabas frowned at her.

"Old Earth joke." She waved a hand. "I found what I think was their cloaking program, but invariably, it's going to rely on pieces of programs that are stored in different places. It's not like every relevant subroutine is going to be labeled 'Cloaking.'"

"Why the hell not?"

"You've clearly never spent any time around programmers. The first few lines are meticulously documented, and it all deteriorates from there. The whole thing winds up being held together with duct tape and bailing wire. It's like that across every species I've ever seen." She grinned and opened her mouth to add another quip, then straightened. "Heads up, the Yennai fleet is incoming."

"Everyone strap in," Barnabas told the rest of the crew. "Shinigami likes to do barrel rolls when she's punchy."

"Is she punchy now?" Jeltor asked curiously.

"She's always punchy," Barnabas said.

"Damn straight I am."

Koel was speaking with the admiral in hushed tones when Lotar arrived on the bridge, looking nauseous. Koel was fully aware that Lotar had had second thoughts. In his youth, Koel would have been uncompromising about the failure such doubt represented. He would have had Lotar transferred to another ship, or perhaps killed. A first-rate mind like that was dangerous if it was not loyal.

Perhaps it was age, or perhaps it was the loss of Uleq and Ilia—a pang went through Koel's chest—but he wanted to guide Lotar. He wanted Lotar to become a worthy heir. There was so much in him that was commendable, after all. He had the instincts to become all that Koel was and more.

Koel did not fear being surpassed. If his successor made the Yennai Corporation more than it had been under his leadership, he had done well. It was what he had hoped for when he chose Ilia.

Ilia would have chewed up Lotar and spat him out, but...

Ilia was dead.

For a moment, Koel felt the wave of blackness he had tried to suppress. He feared it was going to swallow him whole. His children had been his greatest pride and his greatest achievement, and now they were gone and he would never see them again. Never—

He turned back to the window.

He had to remain calm, especially in front of his officers.

The planet grew larger on-screen. It gleamed red in the light from the nearby suns, and Koel shook his head. They had tried to hide from him. They had poked around in everyone's business, cowing those who could not match them in force or technology, and finally they had made a misstep.

They had taken on the Yennai Corporation.

They would never appreciate the depths of their mistake. They would be dead, killed by their ambitions.

Other species would see what had happened here, however, and they would know not to make an enemy of Koel. He gave a thin smile.

"Begin targeting the cities," he instructed. "We will fight the fleet, but first we will show them that they have nothing left to defend. That they failed utterly."

The officers nodded. Their fingers danced over the keys. The Jotun ships were coming into focus now, changing from pinpricks of light gleaming in the darkness to recognizable shapes.

"Sir?" One of the officers scratched his head. "I'm having trouble locating the cities. They aren't where they should be."

"Try a different scanning protocol." Their commanding officer made a show of being involved, leaning over their chairs and pointing at the screens. "The volcanic eruption is throwing off your sensors. The city should be at..." He frowned.

Every one of his team was silent now, staring at their screens.

Koel felt a stab of worry.

"What is it, officer?"

"It's...it's the wrong planet." The officer looked up, too horrified even to find a clever way to say it. "Again. They directed us to the wrong planet. Again. There's nothing here."

On the bridge of the *Shinigami*, the crew burst into laughter. Gar held his side, Tafa leaned on one of the desks, and Jeltor's powersuit shook with mirth.

"They got the wrong data," Shinigami gasped. "And they fell for it. Again." She nodded to Tafa. "All accolades go to our resident artist, who really helped make this fake-out a thing of beauty."

"I am but a humble painter," Tafa protested, but her eyes were dancing.

"We should have one on every ship." Barnabas looked at the screens as one of the sensors whistled. "Ah, yep, there they go. They're arming *everything*."

Shinigami settled back in her seat with a grin. "Showtime."

26

"Destroyers, engage." Admiral Threton's voice echoed over the fleet channel.

Shinigami watched as the first wave of destroyers advanced. After extensive discussion, they had decided to have the ships engage in much the same way as they had before, not visibly adjusting their formations to account for cloaked Yennai ships.

Behind the scenes, they would plan to head off the cloaked ships—but for as long as possible, they would not tip their hand that they had the means to see through Yennai cloaking.

The destroyers had locked onto their targets and were preparing missiles as the carriers disgorged fighters. At the head of the fleet, flying just over Admiral Threton's ship, the *Shinigami* waited.

"It's coming," Shinigami murmured to Barnabas. "Any moment now."

"I suppose we've overlooked an important possibility,"

Barnabas said. He looked worried now. "What if he turns around and leaves? Just heads for a colony and—"

"Nope." Shinigami had cocked her head to the side as if listening to something only she could hear. When Barnabas frowned, she tapped at her ear. "I got a line onto their bridge. Koel is pissed, and he wants us all to die a fiery death. One second, informing the Jotun fleet of his orders."

The Yennai ships advanced quickly with their missiles armed.

"He wants us all dead as quickly and painfully as possible." Shinigami's eyes narrowed. "He's starting to break."

"What does that mean?" Barnabas asked as their ship banked and readied its own weapons.

"I mean that before, Koel didn't give a damn who he hurt. You know how some people hurt others because they like doing it? He wasn't like that. He didn't care about anyone else. He just did what he had to do to get what he wanted."

She shuddered. "I hate him," she said quietly. "I even hate him for what he did to Uleq and Ilia. That doesn't make sense, does it?"

"I think it does," Tafa said. She looked at Shinigami. "That's what happens with people like Koel. They turn on everyone eventually, even their allies, and you wind up sympathizing with...murderers, slavers, torturers. But it's the kind of sympathy that doesn't mean anything. At the end of the day, anyone who throws their lot in with someone like Koel is dangerous."

Shinigami nodded. She turned back in her seat and aimed directly at the *Avaris*, holding the commands in her systems. She wanted to throw everything she had at Koel, tactics be damned. *Try to crack my mind open, you bastard? Try to break me?* ME? *You'll get more than you bargained for.*

But she refused to allow her hatred to push her into stupidity. She aimed one missile at the destroyer nearest the *Avaris,* specifically targeting the area of the ship she guessed held the munitions.

The first impact crackled along the shields but showed her that they were not impervious. She fired three more in close succession, each targeting the same place. The first produced an even more impressive display of electronic feedback, the second actually impacted the hull, and the third broke through. The magazine exploded, tearing the ship nearly in half, and sent it spinning out of control.

There was a cheer from the Jotun ships, and several of their destroyers copied the technique in short order. None of them were willing to waste even a second.

The Yennai ships retaliated at once. Fighters swarmed from the Yennai carriers, as well as the *Avaris,* and dropped in behind the missiles, closing the gap between the fleets quickly.

"Destroyer Group 1, continue your assault on the Yennai destroyers. Destroyer Group 2, focus on Carrier 1."

Shinigami joined forces with one of the Jotun ships to focus on a Yennai destroyer. With the fighters now engaged, getting missiles through would not be so easy. A scatter of cannon fire kept them at bay, but there were so many of them that they resembled a swarm of gnats.

Gnats with guns.

The second wave of Jotun destroyers assembled carefully. Their target Yennai carrier was cloaked, and they did not want to rouse the ship's suspicions.

Shinigami's attention was focused mostly on them, even as she directed her guns at the fighters to help the Jotun missiles reach the destroyer. She watched while Group 2 of the destroyers closed ranks and readied their weapons.

The admiral took control of the destroyers for this maneuver, and the crew of the *Shinigami* watched with their jaws hung open as the destroyers swung in a perfectly timed formation and fired in unison.

The first round of missiles knocked out the shield, and the second set, directed at specific points along the hull, breached the carrier and vented its atmosphere. The ship spun out of control, uncloaking, and razed another destroyer as it went.

"Well, our hand's tipped now," Shinigami murmured. "Let's see what they do."

On the bridge of the *Avaris*, she saw Koel standing white-faced with fury.

He was, however, smart enough not to give specific orders just yet. He allowed his officers to direct the battle as they saw fit.

Dammit. Shinigami would prefer it if he weren't intelligent about any of this. She wanted him to issue nonsensical orders and scream unintelligibly. She wanted him to see his own helplessness and be crushed by it.

Yennai destroyers surged forward and attacked the Jotun formation. They were desperate not to lose another carrier. If the Jotuns extinguished the capital ships and turned on the *Avaris*, the Yennai fleet would be in dire straits.

Shinigami tried not to flinch as Jotun ships were hit.

She fired pucks and missiles of her own to keep the *Shinigami* safe. She maneuvered more nimbly than a human pilot could, but she could not save all the Jotun ships.

She hoped Jeqwar was safe, but she could not bring herself to check.

"Take the last two carriers at once," the admiral ordered. "I will take control of the fleet once you are in position. Move now, regardless of what ships are missing."

Shinigami held her breath as the Jotun ships battled to get into position. Three were taken down as they maneuvered and the resulting formations had gaps in them.

Even after the losses, Admiral Threton did not change his action plan. Shinigami wondered what it must feel like to have the ships missing, not responding as he sent the signals. When the last two carriers were destroyed, she did not smile.

They were doing what they had to do, but the cost was high. It was far, far too high.

On the bridge of the *Avaris*, Koel snarled his fury. They'd broken through his ranks and destroyed his ships. Everything he had built over the course of decades was being taken apart piece by piece.

He glowered at Lotar, who instinctively backed away.

This. *This* was what left of Koel's legacy: this coward, a broken fleet, and the cloud of rubble where Koel's children had met their end.

The void seemed to reach for him, roaring in his ears, and he fixed his eyes on the ships before him.

"Throw everything at them," he ground out. "Use the new missile. Aim it at the *Shinigami*."

"But, sir—" the admiral objected.

"Do it."

"Sir, the carriers are a much more dangerous target than—"

"I said *do it!*" His voice was raw with fury. He grabbed a sidearm from one of the other officers, whom he then sent sprawling. The barrel of the gun came up, pointed at the admiral. It trembled in Koel's hands, but at this range, he wouldn't miss.

The officers on the bridge blanched, and a few ducked under their desks.

Cowards.

"Yes, sir," the admiral said finally. He gave the orders loudly: "Fire the grappler missile at the *Shinigami*."

"Yes, sir."

Koel knew his crew wondered how they'd survive when they had fired everything they had at the *Shinigami* and still had the Jotun fleet to contend with.

It was good that they were wondering. If they didn't guess the truth, the Jotun fleet wouldn't, either.

And when Koel drove the *Avaris* straight into the center of the Jotun fleet, he would leave only rubble in his wake. They would be too close to the planet to pull up at that point. They would be going too fast.

But what did it matter if he survived, after all? Everything he had worked for was in ruins.

My children...

Avaris. Uleq and Ilia. He would be with them soon. Koel swayed as he stumbled to the navigational controls. The officers scattered out of his path, mindful of the gun still in his hand.

"We fought well," Koel told them. "We built something magnificent. This fleet was a thing of beauty. But as you know, strength and power are nothing if they are outmatched. Today, we have found ourselves outmatched." He entered the sequence to accelerate the *Avaris*. "All that is left to us is to make our enemy pay for killing us."

The officers gaped at him. The admiral understood first and ran toward Koel, but Koel leveled the gun at his chest and fired. The admiral's body skidded and fell into one of the recessed bays, and the crew nearby screamed and scrambled away from it.

Koel pointed the gun around the bridge. He laid in coordinates, his eyes meeting theirs. "There is no escaping death now," he told them. "We will die a glorious death together."

The grappler missile soared toward the *Shinigami*, its cables humming with energy. There was no way it was getting away from him.

And then another ship appeared in the space between the Jotun fleet and the *Avaris*. Confused by this new target, the grappler missile altered its course.

"Sir!" The officer's yell was instinctive. "It's a Yennai ship. It's reading as a *Yennai* ship, and the missile is locking on."

"We're here," Tik'ta announced. "Just scanning the area for—"

Her voice trailed off in a squeak.

"Holy *shit*..." Dretkalor breathed. Dwarfing them on either side were entire fleets. Ships had already been lost, their shattered hulks twisting gently in clouds of debris. They had arrived in the middle of some sort of ceasefire, and the silence only made everything even eerier.

The scanners lit up with a wail, and Chofal screamed, pointing.

"It's a missile! It's locked onto *us*!"

"Go!" Zinqued screamed at Tik'ta. "*Go, go, go, go!*"

The officers on the deck rushed to the targeting systems. The crisis had broken through their shock after Koel's orders and Koel stood frozen, staring at the screen. He still held the gun, but even he was so surprised by the sudden appearance of the other ship that pointing it at anyone didn't occur to him.

Lotar took his chance. He tackled Koel to the floor. The gun clattered across the floor, and Koel growled in fury. His hands found Lotar's throat.

"You can't stop this!" There was no sanity left in his eyes.

"You've lost your mind!" Lotar choked out. He struggled against Koel's grip, but the older Torcellan was surprisingly strong. Spots danced in front of Lotar's eyes as his blood flow was cut off. "For the love of all that's holy, do you really want to die?"

Koel threw back his head and laughed. His hands relaxed finally and he rolled away, his cackles echoing off the metal ceilings and floors. Lotar pulled himself away, heaving for breath. He met the eyes of the rest of the bridge crew, but no one knew what to do, seeing their leader run mad.

"Of course, I want to die!" Koel hissed. His gaze swept them all. "What is there left for me? My children are dead. My wife is dead. I have no legacy."

Fury swept through Lotar. He launched himself at Koel, pounding his fist into the other Torcellan's face. He smashed it until Koel's blood streamed onto the metal floor.

"And what about *us*?" Lotar screamed. "What about us? Didn't it occur to you that *we* might want to live? We don't want to die just because you've lost your damned legacy!"

He saw now that Koel had never thought of that. Koel had never once considered his employees as anything more than *things*, there to help or hinder him. To Koel, no one else in the universe was really a *person*. His wife, he had killed because she questioned him. His son, he had killed to strengthen his daughter—and only because his daughter was someone who would help his own legacy grow.

Koel had never cared about anything but his own glory.

Lotar hauled the bleeding Torcellan upright and pushed him toward the console. "Undo the commands! Undo them! Now!"

Koel was still laughing. Even as Lotar had smashed his knuckles into Koel's face, Koel never stopped laughing. He had no sense of reality anymore. He sank to the floor and looked up at Lotar, who shuddered when Koel's eyes fixed on him.

"No," Koel said. "It's under my authorization, and I put it through without overrides. There's no way to undo it now."

The missile streaked closer. Tik'ta pushed the *Julentai* as fast as it would go, but the missile was accelerating. Then the *Avaris* pushed ahead of the rest of the fleet, gunning for the Jotun ships.

"*Go!*" Zinqued screamed. Caught between the planet and the dreadnought with the missile closing in the *Julentai* was impossibly outmatched, but some ridiculous part of him didn't seem to grasp that.

A transmission broke through the static and the wailing alarms. "*Haron's Shield*, this is the *Avaris*." The voice was tight with worry. "Continue evasive maneuvers. We are attempting to reroute the missile."

"Attempting?" Tik'ta shrieked. She hadn't bothered to press the button for transmission, for which Zinqued was grateful. She swerved and threw everything she had into the systems. She didn't have any time to be sending messages.

Chofal worked at the secondary desk. The Yofu didn't bother to run back to the engine room. No changes they could make now would happen in time. She shut down auxiliary systems one by one, and the heat was already climbing.

"*Haron's Shield*, we are doing everything we can. Loop around and try making a pass down in front of the fleet.

We'll try to terminate the missile in the crossfire. Maybe we'll hit some of those Jotun bastards at the same time."

"It's working." Chofal looked dazed. "It's actually working. They think we're a Yennai ship."

"Good," Dretkalor said. "Because that's the only thing that has a chance in hell of saving our asses."

"Holy shit," Shinigami swore. "Everyone out of the way! *Move!*"

"What's going on?" Barnabas asked worriedly. "What's happening with that ship?"

"It's some Yennai ship that showed up late, but that's not the headline here. Koel's gone stark raving mad. He's trying to take as many of us with the dreadnought as he can, and he's not going to pull up before he hits the planet's surface."

"You can't be serious."

She directed her attention to evasive maneuvers while responding, "I am as serious as a poutine shortage in Chicoutimi during a bonspiel. The guy's fucking nuts. Peanut brittle. Cocktail mix with the Chex taken out. Big can of honey-roasted crazy."

Barnabas was laughing. He abruptly stopped, frowned, and leaned closer to the screen. "I'll be damned! Isn't that the ship that tried to capture us before? At the Yennai headquarters, I mean."

"That's ridicu—" Shinigami scanned it. "Sonofabitch. It's showing up as a Yennai ship on the scanners, but it *is* the same ship. I have the technical specifications and the pictures I took last time. "They're... Well, they must be trying to... You know, I have no idea. What *are* they doing?"

"Regretting their life choices?" Gar suggested. He watched as the ship wavered wildly and tried to dive under the nose of the *Avaris*.

"Bingo," Barnabas said. "That. Right there. That's what they're doing. I'd make another speech that would make them wet themselves, but I'm honestly not sure I'm scary enough to outdo a dreadnought."

"You could always *try*," Shinigami pointed out. "You can't just bail every time you get a little competition. All right, everyone, hold on. We're getting out of the way of the *Avaris*, because I'm honestly not betting on anyone being able to override Koel's commands."

"We could ask Koel to," Barnabas suggested.

"Don't have to, actually." Shinigami switched over the screens. "We're being hailed. Looks like Koel wants to make a speech."

———

"*Haron's Shield*, you are clear of the missile. I repeat, you are clear of the missile. Crossfire detected, follow heading 4481 to evade," the communications officer shouted hurriedly into the mic. "We're closing on the planet fast," she whispered to her commanding officer.

At the navigation desk, Lotar had retrieved Koel's gun and pointed it at him while the rest of the crew watched with bated breath.

No one was going to intervene. Koel had gone insane

and shot the admiral. Lotar was only doing what needed to be done.

But it didn't seem to be making any difference. Koel picked up the communications unit, and Lotar screamed with fury. He ordered Koel to undo the commands, and when Koel did not move, Lotar shot him.

Koel did not fall. He stumbled back and looked down at his stomach, where the bloodstain was spreading across his clothes. He looked up at Lotar and smiled.

"Shoot him again," someone whispered. "We have to—"

Koel brought the comm up to his mouth.

"Assembled fleets." He smiled at the bridge crew beatifically despite the blood streaming down his face and staining the front of his robes. Lotar stared at him in horror. They all did. "Today you have witnessed the fall of the Yennai Corporation. Those of you on the Jotun and human ships believe this is your victory, but this is *no* victory, not for anyone. The Yennai Corporation was a marvel, something beyond what others had ever dreamed.

"Others were scared of our vision, the Jotuns and the humans among them. They banded together to destroy us, as lesser creatures will always band together to defeat those who aspire to more. No doubt they now think to put us on trial and hold us to their laws."

Outside the windows, the fiery glimmer of the atmosphere burned. The surface of the planet approached much too fast.

"I will not be used and shamed," Koel told them. "I will not be made into propaganda, reduced to a mere civilian in one of their jails. And I will save my crews as well. I will keep them free of such petty moralizing. We will die with honor!"

Before any of them could stop him, he suddenly lunged at Lotar. Lotar struggled, but Koel snatched the gun and shot the control panel, splintering it, then put the gun to his head, pulling the trigger as the officers backed away.

The *Avaris* sped through the black, hitting the atmosphere with a visible flare of heat. Jotun ships, scattering before it, accelerated full-bore to get out of the way of its massive sides. Shinigami wove between them so as not to hit anyone, and her crew looked at one another, jaws open.

"He's crazy as balls," Gar said finally.

"He— Where did you learn that phrase?" Barnabas blinked.

"Tabitha." Gar watched the dizzying view on the screen as Shinigami swerved and banked. "She tried to explain it, but it didn't make much sense. He really didn't care about any of them in the end, did he? He would rather kill all of them himself than let us 'win' by any stretch of the imagination."

"Yes," Barnabas agreed softly.

"I didn't expect that." Tafa came forward to watch as the *Avaris* smashed into the surface of the barren planet at last, shattering and causing a monumental shockwave. "I thought he would fight to the end. I used to dream of taking away everything Mustafee cared about and making him live as I had lived, but now I'm glad I didn't. What would he have done to the people around him if he'd faced death? He might have killed them like Koel did."

They nodded quietly.

"Radio back to High Tortuga," Barnabas told Shinigami. "The real one this time, mind you." There was the shadow of a smile at his lips. "Tell them the Yennai Corporation is gone. We'll clean up the dregs of it at our leisure."

Shinigami looked at him. "A full report will show my data breach and my internal protocols in that case—"

"I know them," Barnabas said, untroubled. "And I think I speak for everyone when I say, 'don't you dare.'"

"I would have if I could have done so at the time."

"I know that. So I'm glad you couldn't." Barnabas smiled at her. "Also, I have a present for you on High Tortuga."

"What is it?" She looked intrigued now, diverted by the change in topic.

"You'll see when we get there." Barnabas settled back in his chair. "Now for the important question. A game of chess while we make our way there?"

"It depends. Did you clean the blood off the chessboard?"

Among the horde of fleeing Yennai ships now being picked off by the Jotun fleet, the *Julentai* dove around the edge of the planet and accelerated away into the black.

"D'you think the *Shinigami* noticed us?" Chofal asked nervously.

"Of course not," Zinqued declared. They'd gotten away with their lives, and he was absurdly grateful.

Still, he was a bit glum as well. Now they had to come up with a whole new plan to catch the *Shinigami.*

He'd think of something, he decided. He always did.

It wouldn't be long before that ship was theirs.

The sounds of steel drums carried along the sea breeze. Nearby, in a vat of sea water, Jotuns bobbed and darted around one another. Gar thought they were dancing. Shinigami was sure it was a Jotun fight club.

Tafa was painting it.

Barnabas, meanwhile, tried to teach a very unwilling patient how to walk.

"Come on." He held out his hands. "Just one step. You're doing really well."

"You keep it up with that encouraging crap," Shinigami said testily, "and I'll rip your eyes out. I can do it now, too. I have fingers." She took a step, moved the wrong leg the next time, and toppled into the sand.

"Somehow, I'm not too worried about your vengeance." Barnabas grinned down at her. "Do you want me to help you up?"

"I'll crush your throat."

"Uh-huh." He surveyed the ocean as she levered herself up.

She'd been ecstatic when she saw her mechanical body. Barnabas, having conversed with Bethany Anne about TOM's progress, had commissioned an avatar in the image Shinigami most often used—a cross between Tabitha and Bethany Anne.

Tabitha had proceeded to announce that she needed to make sure the ass was up to her standards before she could let Shinigami be installed in the body. Apparently, it had passed muster.

None of them had anticipated how difficult it would be to move in it, however.

"You'd think there would be subroutines for this sort of thing," Barnabas mused.

"There are." Shinigami looked annoyed. "I'm not using them. I should be able to walk on my own, shouldn't I?"

"It takes humans what, a year? More? And even *then* they aren't good at it for—"

"I'm not a baby!"

"Uh-huh." Barnabas was still looking away. Shinigami was very prickly about having anyone help her with this. She'd wanted to have a sparring match with Barnabas as soon as she woke up.

Then she had pushed herself sideways off the bed and shattered a chair by landing on it—not to mention Gar's leg, since he'd been sitting in the chair in question. He was still quite wary around her, which didn't help her mood.

"All right, I'm trying again." Shinigami brushed her dark hair behind her ear—a process that involved hitting herself in the face twice and nearly tangling her fingers in her hair—and took a few shaky steps. "It's easier when I don't think about it too hard for some reason."

"A lot of things are like that."

"Yes, but do you know how hard it is for an AI not to give something their whole focus?"

"Do you remember when you first made an avatar?" Barnabas asked her. He strolled along at her side, his hands behind his back. "You sat perfectly still and never blinked. Now you laugh, you make the eyes look at things you're focusing on, you fidget—all of it. You'll get the hang of this too."

"I suppose so."

"You suppose so? Let's have some verve."

"Fine. I *will* get the hang of this. I *will* crush my enemies and see them driven before me, and hear the lamentations of their women. Happy now, Mr. Show Some Verve?"

"Not quite." Barnabas pulled off his shoes, tossed them into the shade of the trees at the edge of the sand, and waded into the water. He smiled. "Now I'm happy."

"You can't be serious. Why are you wading into the water?"

"It's warm. It feels nice. You have nerve endings, yes?"

"Yes, but I hate them." She shuddered. "Constant biofeedback. Take a step, feel some pain. Adjust your posture, feel some pain. How do humans deal with it without going mad? Actually..." She frowned. "That explains a lot. You're all mad."

"As hatters," Barnabas agreed. "I don't think that's why, but I could be wrong. You're walking very well right now, by the way."

"Am I? I wonder how I'm doing that. I... Oh, sonofa—" She tumbled into the sand. "You say not to think about it, and then you draw my attention to it?"

"Yeah, that one was on me. I'm sorry."

She stuck out an arm and tripped him, sending him sprawling into the waves. "There. Now we're even."

"I liked this coat!"

"I'm sure the saltwater will wash out. Don't be such a baby." She wiggled her toes in the sand. "This feels peculiar."

"It does, doesn't it?" Barnabas sat up but didn't bother to get out of the water. He stretched out his legs and leaned back on his hands, looking at the sky. "You know, aside from the sky being too purple, this is a nice place. I bet we could start a proper resort for humans here."

"You want to run a hotel?"

"No, that sounds terrible. Just a large building for people to visit when they wanted to. I think Tabitha would like it."

"Probably." Shinigami made a few attempts to pull her hair into a ponytail and gave up. "Jeltor's coming."

"How can you tell that's Jeltor?"

"I put a little sticker on his suit when he wasn't paying attention."

Barnabas snorted and bit his lip. "Hello, Jeltor," he said as the Jotuns approached.

"You're getting better at recognizing us!" Jeltor sounded pleased.

"I… Er, yes."

Liar.

I can't admit to him that they all look like blobs of grape jelly to me. He'll be crushed.

Shinigami scowled at him. *You shouldn't lie,* she said primly.

Where is this sudden streak of morality coming from?

She snickered and looked at Jeltor. "So, how is the party going?"

"Very well." Jeltor smiled as fireworks exploded above. "It's not every day you avoid getting crushed to death by a dreadnought, after all.

"And we are drinking in memory of those we lost in the battle."

Shinigami studied her hands. When she had been an avatar, she could just disappear rather than decipher what to do with her expression. She bit her lip.

"Plus," Jeltor continued, determinedly cheerful, "now we have to go back and get hauled up on treason charges by the Senate while *we* try to haul *them* up on treason charges, so we might as well have a good party before we go. We won't be getting any for a while, I think."

"Would you like us to testify?" Barnabas asked him.

"I'd like you to get Gar before he's sick in the pool."

"Dear Lord." Barnabas stood and hauled Shinigami to her feet. "I forgot that we didn't give him the upgrades to make him impervious to alcohol."

"He said he didn't want them. I think Luvendan was a bit on the boring side and he's been wanting to cut loose. You know, get drunk, get in bar fights—that sort of thing."

"I'm going to regret bringing him aboard, aren't I?" They headed off through the trees. "Next time, we go somewhere with no bars."

"If you go somewhere with no bars, how are you going to find trouble to fix?" Shinigami frowned at him.

"There was that distress signal we picked up earlier today—the one from that farming planet. We could start there and see what we find. And you've clearly never lived in a monastery. There's always trouble, regardless of whether there's a dive bar for it to happen in." Barnabas looked at the sky with a grin. "There's *always* trouble," he repeated. "So let's get Gar, feed him some coffee, and go find it."

FINIS

Thank you for reading Paladin! As always, diving into the Kurtherian universe has been amazingly fun, and I can only hope you've had as much fun as I have when writing. With Tafa's recovery, Gar growing into his abilities, and Barnabas and Shinigami forging a true friendship, there's a lot to root for, and that's the type of series you really hope to get to write.

The publishing team has, as always, been amazing. Jeff with his amazing covers, Lynne and her team on editing, Steve helping all of us stay on task, Michael bouncing plot ideas around with me, and the beta readers helping me keep everything tight! I'm lucky to work with this team and in this world.

There's a lot coming up this year: more Dragon Corps, more Barnabas, and (as we go into next year) some more of Nicky's story, as well as a two-book series of steampunky, dragony adventures! I can't wait to share it all with you, so definitely sign up for the mailing list if you haven't already:

https://landing.mailerlite.com/webforms/landing/w0k9j4

Happy reading,

Nat

AUTHOR NOTES - MICHAEL ANDERLE

JULY 24, 2018

First, THANK YOU for reading through both this story to the end and my *Author Notes*.

Just the other day, Natalie reached out through our Slack channel and asked for story ideas for our pals Barnabas and Shinigami, and how we might want to tell them.

I suggested that we go 'on the road.' Of course, it's obvious you can't quite go on the road in space, but the idea is there in principle. So, my version was to go to different areas (maybe space stations?) and track down those messing with people and adjudicating a little Barnabas Justice along the way.

He might swing through and say hi to the peeps from time to time, but this would be the road show for the two of them (and the rest of the team).

BUT, as I considered what to write in these *Author Notes*, I wondered what *YOU* would tell Natalie if she had asked? If you have ideas, why not send them to her? You can find her at her Facebook page here:

https://www.facebook.com/nataliegreyauthor/ .

GO ahead…reach out!

Personally, I hope about thirty (30) of you do this, and pummel her (in a good way) with all sorts of directions you hope to see Barnabas and Shinigami head in!

For those interested, Bethany Anne will be making a return August 10, 2018 (about two and a half weeks from when I'm writing this) and this time, Michael is responsible for a little baby-sitting.

However, there is a reason he was able to last over a thousand years on Earth and it had a lot to do with his ability to see into the future and figure out what he needed to keep his sanity.

(It's a pretty cool solution, and I want one or three myself.)

However, it has a *drawback*, and John Grimes might find out first-hand the challenges of Michael's…toy.

Finally, it's time they get serious about building a barbeque pit, but the Queen has put her size seven-and-a-half shoes firmly down on where she *doesn't* want it, on pain of *pain* if they fail to listen to her.

Will Michael do that? Or, is he truly that stubborn?

Check out the pre-order (sometime soon) to make sure you have it when Amazon drops it at midnight Aug 10th.

I hope your summer is FANTASTIC. We will be publishing another twenty books to keep you up all night and sleeping all day before summer ends!

Ad Aeternitatem,

Michael

CONNECT WITH THE AUTHORS

Natalie Grey Social

Email List

https://landing.mailerlite.com/webforms/landing/w0k9j4

Follow Natalie on Amazon

https://www.amazon.com/Natalie-Grey/e/B01MYG7K8P/

Facebook

https://www.facebook.com/Natalie-Grey-393234677682987/

Michael Anderle Social

Website:
http://kurtherianbooks.com/

Email List:
http://kurtherianbooks.com/email-list/

Facebook Here:
https://www.facebook.com/TheKurtherianGambitBooks/